Big Little Lies by Liane Moriarty - Reviewed

By
J.T. Salrich

CONTENTS

About the author

Liane Moriarty is an Australian author who has written six international bestselling novels, including The Husband's Secret, which has sold over 2 million copies; the film rights have been bought by CBS.

Liane was born in Sydney in 1966, and has been an avid reader since early childhood. Her childhood friends recall how they would hide all their books if Liane came to play, otherwise very little playing would get done.

Liane's early career was in advertising and marketing, where for some years she embraced the corporate lifestyle, before "downgrading" to freelance copywriting for adverts. Spurred on by the fact that her younger sister Jaclyn had a novel published, Liane enrolled in a Master's degree at Macquarie University in Sydney. As part of that degree, she wrote her first novel, Three Wishes, which was published internationally and put her on the road to international literary stardom. She has since written five other adult novels, including this one, the film rights for which have been bought by Nicole Kidman and Reese Witherspoon.

Themes

Domestic violence often lurks beneath the surface of what appears to be a "normal" couple or family, and in the case of children often reveals itself as bullying.

A seemingly happy and carefree group of families turns out to not only have numerous skeletons lurking in various closets, but are eventually all shown up to be not as happy as what they portray.

Symbols

Wealth and beauty are initially seen as perfection, but what lurks beneath?

A single mom is presumed to be immature and careless as a parent, but is she more astute than the overly pre-occupied "proper" moms?

Settings

This modern-day tale takes place in the little seaside town of Pirriwee, on Sydney's Pirriwee Peninsular. This is the sort of town where everybody knows everybody else (or at least thinks they do!).

Beautiful beaches are the backdrop for the quaint-sounding town, with its linear shops, Blue Blues Café (the aroma of whose coffee and muffins one could almost smell); and of course Pirriwee Public School which is the center of the drama.

Short Summary

The story begins at the Pirriwee Public School "Trivia Night" – a fundraising dress-up event – Elvis Presley and Audrey Hepburn. Something dreadful has happened, involving police and ambulances, but WHAT?

We are then taken to six months before the Trivia Night. It is the beginning of a new school year at Pirriwee Public School, and parents are bringing their children to kindergarten orientation.

As Pirriwee is the only school in town, it has to accommodate families from all walks of life, and it is here that we are introduced to the central characters:

> Glittery, well turned-out, forty-year-old Madeline, wife of Ed and mother of Abigail (14, from a previous marriage), Fred (7) and Chloe – 5 going on 25 and starting kindergarten.

> Celeste, exquisitely beautiful (though she doesn't seem to know it, and doesn't wear any make-up), married to the fantastically wealthy Perry. They seem to have the perfect marriage, and definitely have everything money can buy. Celeste is mom to 5 year old twins, Max and Josh.

> Jane, 24-year-old single mother of Ziggy (5). Jane is very thin, wears no make-up and chews on chewing gum continuously.

Then there are the two categories of other mothers – the "Blonde Bobs", who belong to the PTA and always seem to have their noses in everyone else's business' and the quieter "mousy" moms, who try to stay out of everyone's way while doing the best they can for their children. Chief of the Blonde Bobs is Renata, a business executive who employs a French nanny to take care of her daughter Amabella.

At the orientation, Amabella comes out of the classroom crying. A boy had tried to choke her. The teacher lines all the boys up and asks Amabella which one had hurt her. Amabella points to Ziggy, unwittingly setting off a potentially disastrous chain of events.

In the months leading up to the Trivia Night, we discover that all in the little town is not as it seems on the surface.

Madeline is having problems with her elder daughter Abigail, who decides to leave home and live with her father, Nathan. Considering that he had walked out on them when Abigail was 3 weeks old, Madeline is not charmed. To make things worse, Nathan is now married to Bonnie, a seemingly squeaky-clean, vegan yoga teacher; clearly Abigail is taken with Bonnie's lifestyle. Complicating things even further is the fact that Nathan and Bonnie have Skye – a 5 year old daughter who will be starting kindergarten with Madeline's daughter Chloe.

Abigail sets up a website to raise awareness of child marriage and sex slavery. She offers her virginity to the highest bidder.

Celeste seems to have everything – the perfect marriage to a good looking wealthy man, a huge house overlooking the bay, overseas holidays, and all the money she can spend and more. What nobody knows, not even Madeline who is her closest friend, is that her husband Perry hits her.

This is becoming more frequent and more severe, and she doesn't know where to turn. The picture perfect marriage is beginning to develop cracks, as the intervals between Perry's violent acts are getting smaller.

The day before the Trivia Night, Celeste unwittingly embarrasses Perry in front of Madeline and Ed; when they arrive home Perry smashes Celeste's head against the wall, then in remorse brings her an ice pack, tea and pain killers. Unbeknown to Perry, Celeste has been seeing a domestic violence counsellor, who has recommended that she have an escape plan.

Acting on this advice, Celeste has rented and furnished an apartment. After this most recent vicious attack, Celeste resolves to move out with the boys while Perry is away the next week.

Jane has just moved to Pirriwee with Ziggy. Ziggy is excited to be living at the sea, and starting school. The incident on orientation day puts a damper on things for both him and Jane. Renata takes the bullying of Amabella so seriously that she sends out a petition for Ziggy to be removed from the school. Ziggy consistently denies that he hurt Amabella. Jane and her friends believe him, but he won't let on as to who the culprit actually is.

Ziggy was conceived on a one-night stand. Jane has been battling many issues since that night. She confides in Madeline and Celeste that the man tried to asphyxiate her, and virtually raped her. He said many horrible things, which have left her battling her self-confidence and self-image. She confides in them that his name was Saxon Banks, and that he was a property developer from Melbourne. Unbeknown to Jane, Madeline googles him. She ends up showing Celeste, who is devastated to see who it is – Saxon Banks is Perry's cousin; their mothers are identical twins.

Jane takes to doing her freelance bookkeeping work at Blue Blues café, which is much warmer than her little flat, and she befriends the owner Tom who, she has on good authority, is gay. It is only on the day of the Trivia Night that Jane discovers that Tom is not gay. Tom attends the Trivia Night, and it is obvious that there is a mutual attraction.

Things come to a head in the days preceding the Trivia Night. Ziggy ends up telling Jane that the bully is Max, one of Celeste's twins. On the evening of Trivia Night, Josh tells Celeste that Max had been bullying Amabella, but was now bullying Skye.

As they are getting ready for the Trivia Night, Perry answers Celeste's phone and ends up finding out about the apartment. As they arrive at the party, Perry asks Celeste if she is planning on leaving him. She says yes; she also tells Perry about Max being the bully and says it's because he has witnessed more than one of their violent bouts. Perry is devastated and promises to get help as soon as he is back from his next trip.

At the party, the food is delayed and the pink cocktails are flowing. Perry is drinking more than usual, and Celeste can see that his anger is building up. They end up on the balcony with Jane, Madeline, Ed, Nathan and Bonnie. Perry is sitting on a bar stool against the balcony, with the others standing around. Nathan is loudly thanking Perry for the fact that Celeste had paid $100 000 to Amnesty International (under an alias, but Madeline worked it out), to cause Abigail to shut down her website. Perry doesn't know about this "donation", and starts making scathing remarks about Celeste not earning anything, but spending lots of money.

When Jane is introduced to Perry, she tells him that they had already met, but that he had said his name was Saxon Banks. Celeste is shocked, and then angered at how Perry brushes off Jane and tells Celeste it didn't mean anything. She throws her glass of champagne in his face, and he hits her across the face, sending her sprawling. Suddenly everyone realizes that he has hit Celeste before. Bonnie starts yelling, telling him that everyone can see what type of man he is. He is smirking at her, and in her anger she pushes his chest, sending him flying to his death on the tarmac below.

In the chaos that follows, Renata declares that she didn't see what happened. Madeline agrees, and suddenly an unspoken pact is made in which all the participants agree that they didn't see what happened. The police and ambulance arrive. The policeman speaks to everyone, but they all claim to have not seen what happened.

The next morning, Ed is telling Madeline that he cannot lie to the police. She wants him to protect Bonnie by saying he didn't see what happened, but this doesn't sit well with him. Just before Ed is due to meet with the detective, Bonnie declares that she is going to tell the police the truth about what happened, and that no one needs to lie for her.

Bonnie is sentenced to do community service. Abigail moves back to live with Madeline and Ed. Celeste has sold the house and moved with the boys into the apartment. She has set up trust funds for the twins, and for Ziggy who was also Perry's son.

Jane and Tom start up a relationship. Life in Pirriwee goes back to normal, but the school will not be having any more alcohol-fuelled fund raising events.

Chapter 1

Mrs. Patty Ponder is at home in her little house overlooking the Pirriwee Public School grounds. It is the night of the Elvis Presley and Audrey Hepburn dress-up Trivia Night.

She loves living right near the school grounds – hearing the chattering of the children, greeting the mothers who frantically rush in and out with their children. She feels that mothers take their mothering so *seriously* these days.

It is pouring with rain, and yet she can hear a lot of shouting and bad language coming from the balcony of the function room. She had been invited to attend the Trivia Night but had declined. What can they be arguing about? The capital of Guatemala (presuming of course that the Trivia Night questions and answers were in full swing)? "Are you all drunk?" she wonders aloud to her cat, as she strains to hear what is going on.

From her window, Mrs. Ponder could see many Elvises (mostly the shiny white, glittering, plunging neckline jumpsuit variety) and Audreys (mostly the black dress and pearl choker ala Breakfast at Tiffany's variety) gathered on the balcony. Suddenly she saw one Elvis punch another, knocking over an Audrey in the process. The fight continued. Someone shouted "Stop this!" Indeed, she thought, what would your children think?

As she wondered if she should call the police, she heard sirens in the distance, and a woman screaming on and on..........

Analysis

This chapter sets the scene for the book – the frantic "serious" mothering, the underlying discord between the parents, and how it all seems to have come to a head at the Trivia Night.

Study question

Why do you think Mrs. Ponder thinks that mothers take their mothering so seriously as compared to her day?

1.

Chapter 2

It is six months before the Trivia Night.

It is the morning of "The festival of Madeline" – Madeline's 40th birthday. After much morning chaos mostly involving getting 7 year old Fred out of the house, she is driving 5 year old Chloe to the kindergarten orientation. Chloe is very bossy, and Madeline has no fears about her starting school – she will no doubt be in charge before too long.

Madeline notices that the driver of the car in front is texting on her mobile phone. She is so engrossed that she hasn't noticed the traffic light change to green. Despite Chloe's protests that they need to get to school, Madeline gets out of her car to shout at the driver to be more sensible, but all the teenagers in the car laugh at her. Don't they understand they could get killed if they use their phones while driving? She shouts at them and turns back to her own car, but her ankle turns over in her strappy new stilettos, and she falls to the ground.

"Oh calamity", says Chloe – a family statement, and a good description of how the day is turning out.

Analysis

Here we meet Madeline, a central character with a quirky nature – funny, but opinionated and outspoken, and she loves an argument. So like her to take it upon herself to "save the world", one texting driver at a time.

Study questions

Is Madeline setting a good example to Chloe by getting out of the car to shout at the texting driver?

Quotation

"That was almost certainly the moment the story began. With the ungainly flip of an ankle."

Chapter 3

Jane happens to be behind Madeline, on her way to take Ziggy to the kindergarten orientation. She sees the glittery woman, in a blue floaty dress and very high strappy sandals, talking to the people in the car in front. Then she sees Madeline fall, and says "ouch". Ziggy asks her if she hurt herself so she explains about Madeline falling over. He asks if the lady is okay, so she gets out of her car to help. She realizes that if Ziggy hadn't said anything, she would have driven past.

They introduce themselves. As Jane is helping Madeline up, Chloe sticks her head out of the window and shouts at Madeline to hurry up, they are going to be late. Jane notices that Chloe is as well dressed as her mother.
As it turns out they are both going to Pirriwee School, Jane offers to take them.

Analysis

Jane and Ziggy are two central characters. Jane seems always to be preoccupied with her own life and bringing up Ziggy single-handed, and she feels she doesn't often notice things she should or react to them appropriately. Ziggy's concern for Madeline spurs Jane to action, and changes the course of their lives.

Study questions

1. Why does Jane think that Madeline is "glittery"?
2. Would it have been wrong of Jane to just drive past?

Quotations

"No wonder you did your ankle," said Jane. "No one could walk in those shoes!" "I know, but aren't they gorgeous?"

"Glittery mother. Glittery daughter"

Chapter 4

Jane parks Madeline's SUV, then takes Madeline and Chloe with her to the school. Leaving Madeline in the car, she takes the children in to school, and becomes the center of attention amongst the moms, who want to know where Chloe's mum is. Jane loves the school, and feels happy as she returns to Madeline and the car.

Having deposited the children, Madeline invites her to join her for coffee at Blue Blues, where she is meeting Celeste for a birthday celebration.

At Blue Blues, Tom wraps Madeline's ankle in ice, and brings them coffee. While waiting for Celeste to arrive, Madeline and Jane start to get to know each other.
Jane explains how her and Ziggy had decided "on a whim" to move to Pirriwee to be close to the beach. She doesn't tell Madeline that she secretly has misgivings about the decision.
Madeline sympathizes with her for being a single mom, and tells how she brought Abigail up on her own after Nathan left them.
Jane admits that Ziggy's father was a one-night stand. At Madeline's prompting she explains how she supports herself and Ziggy by doing bookkeeping work from home.
At 24, Madeline declares Jane to be even younger than her ex-husband's new wife Bonnie, and jokes that Jane mustn't befriend Bonnie. Jane says she probably won't even meet her, but Madeline explains that Chloe and Skye will be in the same class, and how awkward it is going to be at school functions.

Celeste, whom Madeline describes her "tall, blonde, beautiful and flustered" friend, arrives. Jane feels very plain next to her, but wonders why she is flustered if she's tall, blonde, beautiful and rich.

Analysis

In this chapter we learn more about Madeline and Jane. Madeline is
still angry at her ex-husband for walking out on her and Abigail.
Curiosity gets the better of her as she tries to find out all about Jane.
We are also introduced to Tom, who runs Blue Blues.
We meet Celeste, as flustered as always.

Study questions

1. Why would Jane regret the decision to move to the
   beach?
2. Why will it be awkward for Madeline having Bonnie's
   daughter in the same class as Chloe?

Quotations

"It shouldn't matter. She knew it shouldn't matter. But the fact was that
some people were so unacceptably, hurtfully beautiful, it made you feel
ashamed. Your inferiority was right there on display for the world to
see. This was what a woman was meant to look like. Exactly this. She
was right, and Jane was wrong. You're a very fat, ugly little girl, a voice
said insistently in her ear with hot, fetid breath. She shuddered and
tried to smile at the horribly beautiful woman walking toward them."

Chapter 5

Celeste arrives at Blue Blues and is a little disappointed to find someone else sitting with Madeline. Lately she seemed to not be very comfortable in groups for some reason. She was always worrying about how she came across, but with Madeline everything felt fine. She wonders who the young girl with Madeline is – probably a nanny or an au pair.

Celeste pulls herself together and joins them. Madeline tells Celeste that Jane is a new kindly mom, and they warn her about school politics. Jane is adamant she won't get involved in any school politics, but Madeline and Celeste seem to laugh at that.

Celeste gives Madeline her gift of crystal champagne glasses. Madeline's thought is thank goodness Celeste is so rich, then she chides herself for thinking about Celeste's money.

They start up again about school politics, and they proceed to "inform" Jane and the Blonde Bobs (who seem to run the school). Jane feels a bit insecure about it all. Madeline asks if she's being bitchy, and Celeste says yes. She notices that Jane seems to chew gum and drink coffee at the same time.

Madeline decides they should open the bottle of champagne. Jane says she'll just have a sip, as she is a cheap drunk. Celeste tries to persuade Madeline to keep it for another time, but she insists, as it is after all the "festival of Madeline".

When they get back to the school, Madeline wonders if for once she was wrong about having the champagne – they weren't drunk, but they had obviously bonded, and they had about them the atmosphere of a party.

Analysis

We start to get to know Celeste – very wealthy and beautiful, so why does she seem so guarded? The school politics do indeed seem to be a minefield – one that Jane is determined to stay well away from.

Madeline enjoys a good gossip, and a good time, and even though she is injured she's not going to let that put a damper on her birthday. But was it a good idea to arrive back at the school in party mood?

Study questions

1. Was Madeline right to warn Jane about the school politics?
2. Was it a bad idea to have the champagne?

Quotations

"Champagne is never a mistake. That had always been Madeline's mantra."

Chapter 6

Jane felt euphoric when they arrived back at school to collect the children. She'd only managed about 3 sips of the champagne, but they'd had cupcakes, and a good laugh, and she felt that she had made two new friends. She hadn't many friends her own age since she'd had Ziggy, and her mom was always telling her she needed friends of her own age, or at least other mothers as friends – a support system as it were. She had tried a Mothers' Group before, but it was a disaster. She felt that she could be friends with Madeline and Celeste, though, even though the kindergarten was the only thing they had in common. Unfortunately her euphoria was to be short-lived.

Jane thought the school was magical. Madeline explained how last year's Trivia Night had raised the funds to revamp the playground. All the parents are gathered, waiting for the children to come out. Madeline held court with her ankle propped up on a bench, explaining how she had injured herself while trying to save lives. Jane meets Renata (a Blonde Bob and mother of gifted Amabella), who explains that she has a French nanny to care for the children. Harper (another Blonde Bob) tries to interrupt. Renata presumes that Jane is a nanny or au pair, because she is so young, but Madeline comes to her rescue.

The children come out of the classroom and all seem very happy. Celeste's twin boys are very bouncy, and Ziggy is happy but declares he's ready to go home. Suddenly the teacher asks for everyone's attention. She explains that something had happened to Amabella – it appears one of the boys tried to choke her. She asks if the child who did it would own up, and when no-one does she calls all the boys to line up. Amabella seems very distressed, but not as distressed as her mother Renata. When asked to point out the boy who had hurt her, she points to Ziggy. He denies it, but Amabella won't back down.

Analysis

The "minefield' is well on display as the mothers chat together while waiting for their children. The "magical" atmosphere that Jane feels is about to be shattered by the bullying incident.

Study questions

1. Was it right of the teacher to line the boys up and tell Amabella to publicly point out the boy that hurt her?
2. Why do you think Renata is more distressed than her daughter?

Chapter 7

Madeline thinks to herself "I've just made friends with the mother of a bully". She consoles herself with the fact that is Ziggy had tried to choke Chloe, she would have punched his daylights out. The other parents have stepped back, and Jane is white-faced as she steps up to Ziggy's side. Miss Barnes, the teacher, is asking Amabella if she is sure that it was Ziggy who hurt her. Jane says that Ziggy would never do something like that. Renata tells Ziggy to apologize to Amabella, and he confidently tells her that he hadn't hurt her daughter. "Don't lie", yells Renata. Jane says that Ziggy would never lie, and Renata then asks Jane if she is accusing Amabella of lying.

Miss Barnes is wondering why teachers' training college never covered this kind of thing.

Madeline tries to get involved (so much for the "festival of Madeline" – this is not turning out to be a good 40th birthday), but Renata won't back down. Jane says she can't make Ziggy apologize for something he didn't do. Amabella is trying to tell her mother that is doesn't matter, but Renata is relentless. She threatens Ziggy, saying there will be trouble if he ever touches Amabella again, she grabs hold of Amabella and Juliette (the French nanny) and she storms off.

Ziggy tells Jane that he thinks he doesn't want to go to school anymore.

Analysis
The magical atmosphere has turned into a nightmare as Ziggy is accused by Amabella of bullying her, and pounced on by her mother, Renata.

Study questions

1. Should Jane have insisted that Ziggy apologise to Amabella?
2. Why does Amabella say that it doesn't matter?
3. Why doesn't Ziggy want to go to school anymore?

Quotations

"It doesn't matter, Mummy." Amabella looked up at her mother with eyes still teary. Madeline could see the red finger marks around the poor child's neck. "It does matter," said Renata. She turned to Jane. "Please make your child apologize."

Chapter 8

Five months before the Trivia Night.

Its Christmas morning. Madeline and Ed are still in bed when an excited Chloe comes bouncing in. Abigail sends a text message to say Merry Christmas – it is her father's turn to have her for Christmas, and she informs Madeline that they have all been volunteering at the homeless shelter since 5.30 that morning. Madeline is not happy about the way Bonnie's daughter Skye (who is 3 months younger than Chloe), follows Abigail around adoringly.

Madeline comments on how Bonnie had said she "hates all the crass commercialization of Christmas", and how she had now convinced her lazy 14 year old daughter to peel potatoes at the homeless shelter – she'd never peeled a potato in her life!

And Abigail had described it as a "beautiful experience" and said she "feels so blessed". Madeline can't believe it – she hadn't been able to get Nathan up before 8am on Christmas mornings when they were together, now he's at a homeless shelter at 5.30?

Ed says he'll make her coffee – reminding her why she loves him.

Analysis

Madeline is definitely not happy about Abigail spending time with Nathan and Bonnie – particularly Bonnie, with her vegan diet and yoga classes. How can Nathan have changed so much? Madeline is very relieved to have Ed and a "normal" life.

Study questions

1. Is Madeline right to be jealous of Abigail's relationship with Bonnie?
2. Why does Ed making Madeline coffee remind her why she loves him?

Chapter 9

Celeste wakes up on Christmas morning and looks out at the snowy wonderland in Canada, where they are visiting for the holidays. They had battled to get the boys to sleep, but once they did, they looked out at the snow before having a drink together to celebrate Christmas Eve.

Celeste knows that Perry will be excited to give her a very expensive gift as soon as he wakes up. He loves to give gifts, and he outdid even her in his ability to give thoughtful gifts; she knew whatever he gave her would be perfect. She also knows that once they've had breakfast they will go out in the snow with the boys and make snowmen; Perry will post photos on Facebook – the picture perfect family on the picture perfect holiday. Her life really does have so much joy.

She decides she really can wait until the boys finish high school, before leaving Perry.

Analysis
The picture perfect family on a picture perfect Christmas holiday. The imagery is broken by Celeste's thought that she can wait until the boys finish high school, before leaving Perry.

Study question

Should we believe every picture that we see on Facebook, or do you think sometimes pictures can mask a lie?

Quotations

"Today would be perfect in every way. The Facebook photos wouldn't lie. So much joy. Her life had so much joy. That was an actual verifiable fact."

Chapter 10

Jane wakes up on Christmas morning in the small apartment, with Ziggy in bed next to her. He goes to bed in his own bed every night, and wakes up in hers. They've never worked out how it happens. She had been having a bad dream, in which Ziggy has his foot on her throat and she can't breathe.

She watches him sleeping, and mulls over how one day some woman will wake up next to Ziggy and watch him sleeping. She sometimes felt that he was being shortchanged not having a dad and at least one other sibling. She was doing her best, though.

Her mother is convinced that Ziggy is Poppy (her mother's father) reincarnated, and is always telling Jane that Ziggy will grow up to be the lovely gentle man Poppy was.

As Jane watches Ziggy sleep, she thinks about the incident at the kindergarten orientation. Her mother had been furious when she had told her, insisting that Ziggy would never hurt another child. She called Amabella a silly brat, but Jane said she didn't think Amabella seemed like a brat – her mother wasn't very nice, but the little girl seemed like a sweet child.

"Does anyone really know their own child" she wonders. A small fear lurks in the back of her mind, but she won't let it come forward. Could he possibly have…………..?

Ziggy stirs. "Guess what day it is", Jane says.

Analysis

Jane is thinking about the incident at the orientation day. She has to keep pushing to the back of her mind, dark scary thoughts that perhaps Ziggy has it in him to hurt another child.

Study question

How do you feel about Jane's feelings towards Amabella? Shouldn't she be blaming her for accusing Ziggy even when he is claiming innocence?

Quotations

"He was so beautiful. There was no way he hurt that little girl and lied about it."

Chapter 11

Celeste, Perry and the boys are flying back from Canada. Perry has teased the boys for many years that he has special powers and can fly, and they are eagerly quizzing him as to if he can fly as high as the jet they are in.

Perry looks over to Celeste and says he thinks it's going to be a good year for them. With the boys starting school, she will have more time to herself and he is going to do everything he can to make sure it's a good year. She thinks about how sometimes he says something like that, and reminds her how besotted she was with him in the beginning of their relationship.

Analysis
Perry seems to be relaxed from his holiday, and promises to do all he can to ensure that the coming year is a good one for him and Celeste.

Study question

Why does Celeste feel that perhaps she could stay?

Chapter 12

Four months before the Trivia Night.

Chloe announces that she wants to have a playdate with Ziggy. Ed asks if Ziggy is the boy who – you know (mimics being choked).
Abigail is pushing her steak around her plate – she will later announce that she wants to become vegan, like Bonnie. Abigail says that Chloe should have a playdate with Skye (Abigail's half-sister; Bonnie and Nathan's daughter). Chloe declares that Skye is almost HER sister too – they could be twins like Max and Josh.
Madeline steers the conversation back to Ziggy, saying she'll arrange a date with Jane. Ed says he's not so sure, what if the boy is violent? Amabella did pick him out of the lineup after all. Madeline says that innocent people get picked out of lineups all the time. Ed feels that they should support Renata.

Analysis
Ed feels that since they are friendly with Renata and Geoff, they should support Amabella and not let Chloe play with Ziggy. Madeline feels that Ziggy should be given a chance.

Abigail is about to make things between herself and her mother even worse by deciding to become vegan.

Study question

Should Madeline be supporting Renata, or should she trust Chloe's judgment and allow Ziggy to come and play?

Quotations

"Innocent people have been picked out of police lineups before," said Madeline to Ed.

Chapter 13

Celeste and Perry arrive at the school – the school clothing shop is open for parents to buy the uniforms for the new term. Celeste is feeling fragile – she always does after one of their fights. She had once asked Madeline if she and Ed fought. "Like cats and dogs" Madeline had replied. Perry smiles at her and tells her she looks beautiful in the dress she has on. He is always extra sweet and attentive the day after a fight. "All couples fight", she says to herself.

It had started when the computer she was working on announced a "catastrophic error". She had asked Perry to fix it; after ages it became apparent that he couldn't, and she had said something that upset him. His rage was palpable, and the fight had gone on until they had sex at 5 the next morning (there was always sex afterwards – good sex).

She watched him playing with the boys on the monkey bars. "Did she love him as much as she hated him? Did she hate him as much as she loved him?" were the thoughts going through her head. He had agreed that morning that they should try another counsellor – the one meeting they had previously gone to had not been successful. Perry was away a lot on business – perhaps when he came back from the next trip they would try.

At the clothing shop they bump into Renata. Perry is his usual charming, good-looking self. Renata tells them about the incident with Ziggy, then apologizes to Celeste, saying she knew that they had celebrated Madeline's birthday with Jane. Renata declares that she has told Amabella to stay away from Ziggy. Perry says they should tell their boys the same thing – wouldn't want them getting in with the wrong crowd from the start.

Celeste thinks it is all over the top – the children are only 5 years old! She winces when one of the twins pulls on her arm. Perry knows why, but there are never any bruises to be seen. She knows there will be an expensive item of jewelry for her when he returns from his trip – something to add to the collection she never wears.

Analysis

After a particularly bad fight, Celeste has to put on a brave face at the school. Perry, as usual, is more loving and attentive towards her.

Renata tells Celeste and Perry that she has told Amabella to stay away from Ziggy. Perry thinks he'll do the same – wouldn't want his boys to get involved with a bully.

Study question

1. The parents seem to be quick to want to pick sides, or at least stay on "the right' side. What do you think about this?
2. Explain the irony in Perry wanting to warn the boys about staying away from Ziggy.

Quotations

"My husband hits me, Renata. Never on the face of course. He's far too classy for that. Does yours hit you? And if he does, and this is the question that really interests me: Do you hit back?"

Chapter 14

Madeline calls Celeste to let her know she has arranged a playdate with Chloe and Ziggy. She suggests Celeste should bring the twins. Celeste recounts the conversation with Renata at the school. Madeline gets very angry (she does love conflict!), and tells Celeste that Renata has no right to say anything like that, especially since they don't know for sure that Ziggy was the culprit. Celeste seemed to drift off somewhere as she replied.   Madeline recalls that this was one of Celeste's strange characteristics. She met Celeste when the children were all at swimming lessons. One of the twins had fallen into the pool without either Celeste (who was staring off into space) or the instructor noticing. Madeline jumped in fully clothed and saved him. Celeste was obviously very grateful; they both took their children out of the swim school and ex-lawyer Celeste had written a letter demanding full compensation for Madeline's outfit. They had been friends ever since.

Chatting on the phone, Madeline remarks on how tired she feels and looks all the time. She tells Celeste that Bonnie had been round to pick up Abigail – she describes Bonnie as looking like "a Swedish fruit picker", and how Abigail had run out of the house as if she couldn't wait to get away from her mother.

Analysis

Madeline arranges the play date with Ziggy, and suggests that Celeste bring the twins. She explains how incensed she was about Renata's remark at the school. Amidst all this, she has to worry that she is losing Abigail to her stepmother.

Study question

Why do you think Celeste was so preoccupied that she didn't notice Max fall into the swimming pool?

Chapter 15

Jane and Ziggy arrive at Madeline's house for the playdate. Ziggy says he would love to live in a "double decker" house like this one. Jane reflects on how little Ziggy actually asks for. How different her life would be without him. She ponders on how the doctor told her that her endometriosis was so bad she would battle to conceive. Somehow a one night stand managed it for her.
Although dressed like a 1950s housewife in her red and white polka dot dress and sparkly red ballet pumps, Madeline can't get over the fact that Jane actually baked muffins from scratch. She tells Jane that Celeste and the boys are coming over. They talk about Jane's move.

Jane mentions that she saw one of the Blonde Bobs (she thinks it was Harper) at the gas station, and that Harper had pretended not to see her. Madeline explains that Harper is very loyal to Renata, almost as though Renata was a trophy to be proud of. Madeline wants to call her straight away and demand to know why she ignored Jane. Jane manages to stop her. Madeline says that she won't stand for any of "those women" treating Jane badly because of what happened at the orientation. Jane said she would have made Ziggy apologize if she thought she was guilty, but she's 99 percent sure he was not. As she starts to think back to the night he was conceived, she almost wants to confide in Madeline, but is interrupted as Abigail comes in, announcing that she is going to spend the night at her father's. Madeline is furious, as Abigail hadn't asked her. Abigail can't understand why asking Dad isn't the same thing, and says that she is not a possession that they can fight over.

Ed and Fred come in from surfing, and Ed chats to Jane while Madeline sees to the children. Ed ends up telling Jane that he has loved Madeline since they were children, and was devastated when she married Nathan. A few years later, he happily bumped into her at a barbecue and the rest, as they say………

Celeste arrives and Jane thinks to herself – "great, now I'll be in the presence of both great love and great beauty." She feels insignificant.

Analysis

Jane and Ziggy arrive for the play date. She ends up in the middle of a typical family day – Abigail causing drama, Ed and Fred getting home from surfing, Ed telling the story of how he and Madeline met. Jane feels a bit lost.

Study questions

1. Should Abigail ask Madeline before making arrangements with her father?
2. Why does Jane feel colourless or insignificant?

Quotations

"Great, thought Jane, continuing to pretend-sip her empty mug of tea. Now I'll be in the presence of both great love and great beauty. All around her was color: rich, vibrant color. She was the only colorless thing in this whole house."

Chapter 16

That night as they were preparing for bed, Madeline asks Ed what he thought of Jane. He answers that he can't get used to thinking of her as a fellow parent as she's so young. Madeline thinks she's not as young at heart that they all think, maybe even a bit old fashioned.

Madeline says she'd like to give Jane a makeover – change her hair that is pulled so stiffly back from her face. She also thinks they need to find Jane a boyfriend.

Madeline muses that although they seem so different, Jane and Celeste are actually quite similar, but she can't put a finger on it. Ed says it's because they are both damaged. Jane being damaged Madeline can accept, but Celeste? "What does she have to be damaged about?" Madeline said that she was damaged when Ed met her – he disagrees, saying that she was heartbroken, not damaged.

Madeline thinks back to when she and Abigail had been alone after Nathan left them. How she had done her best to make a good life for Abigail even though her father hardly ever paid maintenance and didn't seem to care about them. Now it seemed as though Nathan was trying to take Abigail away from her. She childishly says that Abigail is meant to love *her* best. Ed jokingly asks id Madeline would like him to bump Nathan off, and frame Bonnie for it.

Analysis
Talking about Jane, Madeline thinks that Jane and Celeste are quite similar, but she can't work out why she thinks that.

Madeline feels that she is losing Abigail to Nathan and Bonnie, which isn't fair since she had brought Abigail up on her own.

Study questions

1. Is there a difference between being damaged and being heartbroken? If so, what?
2. Should Madeline be feeling the way she is about Abigail? Could this just be a phase?

Quotations

"Do you want me to kill the bastard? Bump him off? I could frame Bonnie for it." "Yes please," said Madeline into his shoulder. "That would be lovely."

Chapter 17

It's the first day of school. Jane's parents have come to see Ziggy on the big day. In the schoolyard, Bonnie offers to have Nathan take a family photo of Jane, Ziggy and her parents. Jane thinks to herself how different Bonnie looks to the other parents. She gets introduced to them and Skye.

Just then Amabella marches up to Skye, asks her name, and flips through a pile of pink envelopes looking for Skye's name. Jane's mother comments on Amabella being able to read, to which she replies that she has been reading since she was three. She announces that the envelope is an invitation to her 5th birthday party – an A party since her name begins with A.

Amabella notices Ziggy, clutches the pile of envelopes to her chest and runs off. Jane notices that every other child she can see is holding a pink envelope.

Analysis

Jane meets Bonnie, and notices how differently she dresses to everyone else.

Amabella pointedly omits to give Ziggy an invitation to her party – what is this going to mean for the future?

Study questions

Is it significant that Amabella runs off without giving Ziggy an invitation?

Quotations

"I thought there might have been a certain, I don't know, etiquette about handing out party invitations. I thought what happened on that first day of kindergarten was kind of inappropriate."

Chapter 18

It's the first day of school, and Madeline is suffering from a severe bout of PMS – the one day in every month when she had to *pretend* everything. They arrived at school, where parents were standing around chatting while the children ran around with excitement. Madeline sees Nathan taking the photo of Jane's family. She sees Skye, and notices how certain mannerisms are just like Abigail's. This does not help her mood at all.

Nathan turns and comes to greet them, remarking what a big day it is, and a first for him, although Madeline and Ed were "old hands" at starting children off at school. In her mood, Madeline can't resist reminding him that Skye was not the first of his children to start school. Although embarrassed, Nathan asked if he and Bonnie could have Abigail on the weekend instead of the following one, as they were going to see Bonnie's mother. Bonnie added that Abigail and her mother have a very special connection. Madeline is fuming.

Jane comes over and introduces her parents. Chloe comes up and asks Madeline to keep her pink envelope – the invitation to Amabella's party. Jane's mother mentions that apparently Ziggy is not invited to the party. Madeline is furious and Jane embarrassed. As Madeline turns around she sees Celeste arriving, and Renata handing her two pink envelopes.

Celeste was not having a good morning. Perry was away, and the boys were being difficult. She had battled to get them ready. When she arrives at school, she notices two dads almost fall over some bags as they look at her. She thinks to herself that perhaps she should have an affair.

As they arrive, the twins see Chloe and Ziggy and go running off to meet them. Renata comes up to Celeste, remarks on Perry being away again (she had Googled him, by the way). She hands the two pink envelopes to Celeste, explaining what they are, and that the parents are more than welcome to come along, so that they can all get together.

Madeline comes along, cheeks flushed and with a dangerous glitter in her eyes. She thanks Renata for the invitation that Amabella had given to Chloe. Renata pretends that Amabella took the invitations out of her bag, and that she, Renata, was meant to be handing them out discreetly to the parents. Madeline mentions that it seems everyone except Ziggy was invited. Renata offhandedly asks if Madeline really expects her to invite the boy that assaulted her daughter. Madeline tries to get her to see sense, but Renata is adamant. Madeline then declares that she is *so sorry*, but Chloe won't be able to make it to the party. Renata says she thinks she should leave before she says something she'll regret.

Analysis

The minefield of school politics is about to become more dangerous as Amabella hands out party invitations to all the children except Ziggy.

Study questions

Do you think it was intentional that Amabella handed out the invitations, or did Renata really not notice that she had taken them out of her bag?

Quotations

"This is war, Celeste," she said happily. "War, I tell you!"

"Oh, Madeline," sighed Celeste.

Chapter 19

On the way to Blue Blues to have coffee with Jane and her parents, Ed tells Madeline that she can't make Chloe miss the party just because Ziggy isn't invited. Madeline's mood is not improving, and having to make small talk with her ex-husband and his new wife had not helped. Also, she sympathizes with for Jane being a single mother, remembering how hard it had been bringing up Abigail on her own. How hard it must be for Jane, knowing Ziggy was the only child not invited.

Jane's mother, Di, asks Madeline to walk on the beach with her while the others go into the coffee shop and order. She wants to chat to Madeline about Jane, and thank her for taking Jane under her wing. She is worried about Jane – she has lost a lot of weight lately, her and Ziggy have moved around a lot and she doesn't have many friends her own age. She hasn't had a boyfriend since before Ziggy was born. Di is worried that Jane may have an eating disorder or something, and she feels that Jane doesn't talk to her anymore – it's as though the real Jane has checked out of her mind.
As Jane calls them to come and have their coffee, Madeline promises to keep an eye on Jane.

Analysis
Parental worry abounds as Ed worries about Madeline not letting Chloe go to Amabella's party, Madeline worries because her baby has started school, and Di worries about Jane's state of health and mind.

Study questions

Why would Jane's mom ask Madeline to keep an eye on Jane?

Chapter 20

Its 11am on Ziggy's first day of school, and Jane is doing her freelance bookkeeping at her dining room table, and wondering how Ziggy's getting on. She's battling to reconcile the paperwork for Perfect Pete's Plumbing, and her thoughts turned to all the pink envelopes – so many of them, but not one for Ziggy. She felt hurt for him, and somehow responsible.

Madeline had told her that she had informed Renata that Chloe wouldn't be going. Now Jane felt even worse – Madeline had declared war with Renata over her!

Jane's father had said not to worry, it would all blow over in a week; Ed said or it would blow up now that Madeline was involved.

Battling to concentrate on her work, she wondered what she would post on Facebook if she was that way inclined – something about Ziggy being left out. But she couldn't shrink this down to a Facebook status and hope it would go away. And her mother seemed so disappointed in her. Maybe she should even consider going on a date to make her mother happy. Her cousin had offered to put her in touch with a friend, so she texted "yes, please!" Suddenly her mind flipped back to that night, she felt nauseous, and called her cousin to say that it was a mistake, not to do anything. Too late, declared the cousin.

Analysis

Jane is trying to keep it all together – caring for Ziggy, providing for them both, and being the sort of daughter her mom doesn't need to worry about.

Study questions

Should Jane go on a date just to make her mom happy?

Quotations

"This will all blow over in a week," her father had said at coffee this morning when they were discussing the party. "Or it will all blow up," said Madeline's husband, Ed. "Now that my wife is involved."

Chapter 21

Jane and Celeste are both early for pick-up time. They chat on their way to the school grounds. Celeste knows that Jane supports herself and Ziggy by doing bookkeeping from home. Jane asks her if she would go back to work now that the boys are at school. Celeste explains that she was a lawyer before, and Jane comments that she was supposed to have been a lawyer. Celeste goes on to say that she doesn't need to work, as Perry is a hedge-fund manager and earns very well. She hopes she hadn't sounded as though she was showing off. If Madeline had been there she would have made an off-hand comment about Celeste being able to live a life of leisure, and then she would have followed it up with a comment about how bringing up twin boys is hardly a life of leisure.

Jane and Celeste chat about their mutual lack of exercise, and agree to walk together around the headland every morning when they drop the children off at school.

Madeline was getting ready to fetch the children from school when her boss called. She worked part-time doing marketing for the Pirriwee Theatre. Her boss mentioned that she had a lot of free tickets for Disney on Ice at the Theatre on Sat 28th. Even as Madeline realized it was the day of Amabella's party, she heard herself saying "I'd love them."

Analysis
We get to know more about the lives the women lead, and Madeline does a very Madeline thing in accepting the tickets to the show.

Study questions

Should Madeline have accepted the tickets?

Chapter 22

Celeste and Perry are enjoying an evening of TV watching together, with red wine and chocolates. Perry asks Celeste if they are going to "some kid's birthday party" tomorrow. Celeste replies that they were supposed to be going, but she was taking the boys to Disney on Ice instead, as Madeline had free tickets for a group of them. Perry asked if he was not welcome at the Disney thing, and Celeste suddenly realized that she had made a big mistake. Perry grew angry, saying that he was going away again soon and had been looking forward to some family time. Celeste replied that she had thought he would like some time to himself, perhaps to go to gym. Perry was hurt. Celeste also realized that they didn't *need* free tickets, and that perhaps she had deprived some poor mom from being able to take her kids. As she got up to apologize, Perry grabbed her arm.

She could feel him making a decision. The first time he had hit her, the twins had only been 8 months old. He had promised it would never happen again. But it kept happening, and she kept staying with him. She felt that each time she didn't leave him, she gave him tacit permission to keep on doing it. The problem was that she loved him, was *in love* with him, and when he was in a good mood they had such good times together. Perhaps it was all her fault – she wasn't careful enough about what she said and did.

He let go her arm, and said he was so sorry. There was no one to comfort her. And she wouldn't be able to wear that sleeveless dress tomorrow.

Analysis
Domestic violence rears its head as Celeste "says and does the wrong thing" and angers Perry.

Study questions

Was Celeste truly thoughtless, or did Perry overreact?

Quotations

"She turned her head, took a step away, but there was no one else there to comfort her. There was only him. The real him. She stepped forward and laid her head against his chest."

Chapter 23

Disney on Ice – the children were so excited. Ziggy was clutching Harry the Hippo – the class stuffed toy that went home with a different child each weekend. The lights went off, the music started and the children were spellbound – faces concentrating on the action. Madeline noticed, though, that Celeste had her head in her hands.
All Celeste could think about was "I have to leave him".

Jane is chatting to her mom on the phone. Her mom keeps bringing up Zach, the boyfriend Jane had had before she fell pregnant with Zach. Jane knows her mom still suspects that Ziggy is Zach's son, but Jane vehemently denies it. Suddenly Jane has a thought, grabs Ziggy's bag and turns it upside down – to no avail. Harry the Hippo has been left behind at the theatre.

Jane calls Madeline in tears, to tell her that Harry had been left behind. She's called the lost property line at the theatre, but it seems that Harry has well and truly vanished.

Analysis
Jane has something else to concern her now that the class toy has been lost.

Study questions

Is Jane's mom being a helpful mom, or unwittingly making things difficult for Jane?

Chapter 24

Two months before Trivia Night.

Madeline is getting Fred and Chloe ready for the school athletic carnival. Abigail comments that she's sure Bonnie will win the mothers' race, as she's "so into yoga and stuff". Ed warns her, but Madeline is quite good natured about it, until Abigail accuses her of being too competitive with Bonnie – it's not as if she wants to be married to Nathan anymore. Abigail has a teenage tantrum about not being able to say what she wants to in her own home, Fred is yelling for Madeline, and Chloe is yelling at Fred. Then Abigail comes out with it – she has decided she wants to go and live with Nathan and Bonnie. Madeline has feared this for so long – they had been the Mackenzie Girls! She stared at Abigail, willing her to remember, but she just said "that's what I want".

At the Carnival, Madeline bumps into Nathan and Skye. He asks her if Abigail has spoken to her. Madeline refuses to give him the satisfaction of seeing her upset, so she says its fine with her. Nathan then tells her they'll have to work out a money arrangement, which has her taken aback. He suddenly realizes what he has said, and starts to apologize for all the years that he didn't help Madeline financially in bringing up Abigail.

The kindergarten moms are called for their race, and Madeline finds herself lined up with the 24 year old Miss Barnes, and Bonnie – older, but still younger than Madeline.

Analysis
This chapter highlights the underlying competition between Madeline and Bonnie.

Study questions

Why do you think Abigail wants to go and live with Nathan and Bonnie?

Quotations

"Why did you have to move here, Nathan?" she sighed.

Chapter 25

Jane lined up with the other kindly moms for the race. She had been trying so hard to fit in with the other school moms – she did canteen duty and she helped with reading practice. She chatted with everyone at drop-off and pick-up, but she still felt that she was being judged over the incident at the orientation day. She tries to tell herself that this is small stuff, compared to what happened *that* night.

The other moms were chatting away – a petition was going around against children bringing cupcakes to school on their birthdays, and there was an argument about that. Madeline noticed how "professional" Bonnie looked, in her yoga outfit. The starter gun went off.

Analysis
The school has unwittingly pitted the mothers against each other – it may just be a race, but does it mean something more?

Study questions

Is Jane right in feeling as though she's being judged?

Chapter 26

Celeste and Renata are holding the finish line tape between them. Renata is making small talk with Celeste – she made a point of ignoring Jane and Madeline if she bumped into them at school, but she was treating Celeste as an old friend who had wronged her but whom she had chosen to forgive.

All Celeste could think about was last night. It had started as an argument about the boys not picking up their Lego. Perry had said she was spoiling the boys. She carried on folding the washing and said that if it upset him so much he should pick it up himself. He picked it up, and then came and upended the entire crate of Lego over her. They had ended up slapping and scratching each other. When Perry got up this morning, he had been cheerful, and made a joke when Josh asked him where he got the scratch on his neck. She had had to tell the boys that she fell on the stairs last night and was not able to run the race. She couldn't get Perry's look out of her mind – did he think their behavior was normal or funny?

Madeline touched the line first, closely followed by Bonnie. "Bonnie by a nose", shouted Renata. Celeste insisted that Madeline had won. So now it had come to this – a standoff as to which mother had won, depending on whose side that mother happened to be. One of the Blonde Bobs suggested that they call it a tie, but Madeline looked Bonnie in the eye and said absolutely not - "You beat me fair and square."

Analysis

While Celeste is dealing with her own demons, the competition between Madeline and Bonnie takes a new turn. In this race, at least, Madeline lets Bonnie take the crown.

Study questions

1. Is Celeste at fault for throwing Lego back at Perry and thereby starting the fight?
2. Why do you think Madeline "gave" the victory to Bonnie?

Quotations

"See there? Again. Celeste at fault. She behaved like a child. It was almost laughable. Slapstick. Two grown-ups throwing things at each other."

"You beat me, Bonnie." She met Bonnie's pale blue eyes and saw understanding register. "You beat me fair and square."

Chapter 27

Celeste arrived home from the carnival to find that the house cleaners were there. Her mother could not believe how much she paid them to clean the house – she had always cleaned her own house, and offered to help Celeste with hers. She had never got used to Perry's money.

Celeste heard the cleaners – a married Korean couple – laughing and joking upstairs, and suddenly envied them their easy relationship.

Celeste sat at the computer and donated some more of Perry's money to charity, as if that would ease her pain. But all she felt was a terrible guilt, and that she deserved to be hit. She didn't know if the amounts she pledged would hurt Perry financially – he controlled that side of things. What she did know was that she would never be brought to tears by an electricity bill as Madeline had been that week. Perry never questioned how she spent the money, in fact he often told her she could spend more, and kept reminding her that they could afford new things, but she never really got used to it, especially since she'd stopped working. Sure, she was contributing to their lives by running the home and caring for the boys, but she didn't spend Perry's money the way she would have spent her own.

The doorbell rang – a florist delivering a huge bunch of flowers with a note from Perry to say he was sorry and he loved her. Her hands were shaking, she didn't want the flowers. She thought back to the year she met Perry. "You know what you have to do", she told herself. She sat down in front of Google and typed the words – Domestic Violence.

Analysis
Celeste tries to ease her own pain, and possibly make some for Perry, by donating a huge amount of money to charity. But does it help?

Study questions

Explain the different emotions Celeste is dealing with. Is she handling things well?

Quotations

"See there? Again. Celeste at fault. She behaved like a child. It was almost laughable. Slapstick. Two grown-ups throwing things at each other."

Chapter 28

Madeline is packing Abigail's clothes for her move to Nathan's. Last night Abigail asked if she could take her four poster bed with – it had been a gift for her 14th birthday, from Madeline and Ed. Ed had said no, but Madeline said that since it was Abigail's bed, she could decide. Nathan was coming to fetch it later. Ed pops his head in the door and says that Abigail should be doing her own packing – "surely she's old enough".

Madeline has always felt that Ed expected too much of Abigail. He hadn't been there from the beginning as he had with Fred and Chloe, and so wasn't always reasonable in his expectations as far as age-appropriateness was concerned. When Nathan came back on the scene when Abigail was 11, Abigail had changed overnight in her attitude towards Ed, almost as though she felt that if she was nice to Ed she was betraying her father.

Ed asks if Madeline thinks it's his fault that Abigail wants to move out; Madeline says of course not. She shoos him out, as he has an interview to go to – Pirriwee's oldest book club. Madeline thinks that maybe she should start a book club.

Analysis
Madeline is hanging on to Abigail till the last, by packing her clothes for her move to Nathans.

Study questions

How would you feel if you were Ed?

Chapter 29

Its one month before the Trivia Night.

Ziggy's in the bath. Jane is sitting on the bathroom floor reading the book club book – a romantic novel. She is reading a steamy sex scene, and finds herself starting to get aroused for the first time in ages. Suddenly the old memories from the one night stand threaten to come back, but she pushes them away – she has other memories of sex, normal sex on a normal bed, and she wills those memories to come back.

Ziggy breaks into her thoughts and tells her that he needs to hand in his family tree project tomorrow. She says that it's not due until next week, but then has second thoughts and checks the calendar on the fridge – it IS due tomorrow, and although she has all the photos ready she doesn't have cardboard or other supplies. She is frantic, not knowing how they are going to get the project done in time. She texts Madeline to ask if she has any cardboard at home that she could pick up.

Ziggy doesn't want to get out of the bath, and he and Jane end up having a fight when she pulls out the plug (which he likes to do), and takes him out. He hits her and says he hates her, but then he starts to cry and curls up in a ball. At that moment the doorbell rings – it's Madeline with some cardboard for Jane. Jane bursts into tears.

Analysis
Jane is battling to keep it all together.

Chapter 30

Madeline is keen for an excuse to get out of the house. Abigail has been living with her dad for 2 weeks, and Madeline misses her. They would have been watching TV together right now – Nathan and Bonnie don't even have a TV set. Apparently they all sit around and chat and listen to classical music. When Bonnie comes home to Madeline for a weekend, all she wants to do is watch TV and eat popcorn, and because Madeline is now the "treat giving" parent, she lets her.

Madeline helps Jane get Ziggy ready for bed, then they start on the project. Ziggy has to draw the tree, then he can go to bed with Jane sticks the photos on.

Ziggy says that Miss Barnes told the children they have to put names for both of their parents, even if they don't have a photo they still need to put a name. Jane tries to distract him by pointing to all the pictures of the other men in his life, but he is adamant that he has to show his dad – he points to the example Miss Barnes gave them of a perfect nuclear family. Ziggy is starting to become hysterical, but Madeline rescues the situation by telling him he just has to write "Ziggy's dad". (Madeline thinks she will have to speak to Miss Barns about this – there are other types of families too these days). He obeys, and Madeline puts him to bed with a story.

When Madeline comes back into the room, Jane is busy sticking the photos on the tree. She says that she has always wanted to be truthful with Ziggy about his dad, but it's hard for such a little one to understand. Madeline asks what the dad's name is, and Jane says Saxon Banks. Madeline asks if Jane has ever tried to stay in touch with him and Jane says no, because "Saxon Banks was not a very nice fellow." Madeline picks up that Jane is upset, and she says "Oh, Jane, what did that bastard do to you?"

Analysis
Madeline saves the day twice, by arriving with the cardboard, and by helping Jane deal with a hysterical Ziggy.

Study questions

Describe the difference between the parenting stresses each of these moms are going through.

Quotations

"Because Saxon Banks was not a very nice fellow," said Jane. She put on a silly, posh voice and held her chin high, but her eyes were bright. "He was not a nice chap at all."

Chapter 31

Madeline asks if Jane would like to tell the story.

Jane explains how she and Zach had broken up 3 weeks before, and her friends urged her to go out with them and have a good time to help her forget about Zach. They went to a bar, and met two out-of-town businessmen. They kept buying the girls big expensive cocktails. Saxon Banks took a liking to Jane, and soon she was in the lift with him, going up to his room. He was charming and funny, and made her laugh.

They get to the room, and he pours champagne. They have a drink, and then he takes hold of her. She's not afraid or anything, she's there to have sex with him after all. She helps him undress her and they fall onto the bed. Then he asks her if she's ever "tried this', and starts to choke her. She feels as though she's drowning, and he lets go, laughing. Telling her it can be an acquired taste and that she just needs to relax, he starts choking her again. She's making strange gagging sounds, and wants to cry. He gets angry and says "You're a boring little bitch, aren't you? Just want to be fucked. That's what you came here for, hey?" He forces himself into her and starts saying things into her ear – about her being fat and ugly, with smelly breath. She lies there just staring at the down lighter in the ceiling, feeling as though she's been anaesthetized. He finishes and asks if she wants to watch TV. She gets dressed and leaves.

Analysis
The truth comes out about the "one night stand", and quite a few things become clear.

Chapter 32

Madeline is really sorry for Jane.

Jane says that she should have taken a morning-after pill, but her doctor had told her that she would battle to fall pregnant as she had severe endometriosis. When she realized that she was pregnant, it was much too late for an abortion. Her grandfather had just died and she became severely depressed. She would dwell on the things he had said to her while he was busy on top of her.

Madeline urges Jane not to think that she is in any way to blame. What he did was verbal and sexual abuse. Jane says that some people are into erotic asphyxiation, and she should have been more sensible than to go off with a man she had just met in a bar.

Jane explains how she had been overweight at the time – she had always loved food. He had called her a "fat, ugly little girl". She shows Madeline a photo that was taken a couple of months before the incident. Madeline declares that Jane was not fat, she was curvy. Jane says that the words hurt her so badly because she was naked and vulnerable, and she's furious with herself for letting him have so much power over her.

Jane tells how after that night she couldn't eat without thinking about his words, and her throat would close up as though his hands were over it – a very effective diet, she jokes. Madeline recalls a remark that Jane's mom had made on the beach, and wonders if she is not also to blame for Jane's poor body image.

Jane also explains that she doesn't have bad breath – she's checked with her dentist many times but still feels compelled to chew gum constantly.

Jane reveals that she's not sorry about the night, because she got her "miracle baby' Ziggy. But she does worry about Ziggy having inherited his dad's violent side – she couldn't believe it when Ziggy had been accused of choking Amabella on orientation day! Of all the things – choking. Madeline assures her that Ziggy is a sweet little boy. She asks Jane if she knows where Saxon Banks is now, but Jane doesn't. Madeline says that one could always Google him, but Jane says she actually doesn't want to know, and begs Madeline NOT to Google him.

Analysis
We learn more about how the one night stand has affected Jane's psyche.

Study questions

1. Do women allow men to have too much power over their self-image?
2. Why is it significant that Ziggy was accused of *choking*?

Quotations

"Choking. I couldn't believe it. And sometimes I feel like I can see something in his eyes that reminds me of, of him, and I think, 'What if my beautiful Ziggy has a secret cruel streak? What if my son does that to a girl one day?'"

Chapter 33

Celeste has finally gone to see a domestic violence counsellor –
someone on the Pacific Highway, far from where anyone could
recognize her going in or out.

Celeste is having second thoughts about being there. She had worn a
dress that Perry bought her in Paris, and had put on makeup, in an
attempt to show that she was somehow superior to other women. The
counsellor, Susi, seems very young. Celeste had told her in a quiet low
voice what had been going on. Next, the counsellor asks her if there are
any weapons in the house, and if Perry is ever abusive to the family
pets. Celeste wants to scream "it's not like that, this dress is from Paris,
and my husband drives a Porsche!" She takes pains to get Susi to see
that they both are violent, not just Perry. Susi says that no woman
deserves to be abused. Celeste says she doesn't think she deserves it,
but she's not a victim because she hits him back. Susi asks Celeste if she
has ever been afraid that she will die. She starts to say no, but then
recalls an incident when Perry had pushed her face into a corner of the
couch and almost suffocated her.

Susi asks about the twins – has Perry ever……. Celeste is adamant that
he is an excellent father, who took 3 months off when the twins were
born premature, to help her. Celeste assures her that the violence does
not affect the boys at all, as they have never witnessed anything and
they are just a normal happy family.

Susi seems not convinced, and asks Celeste if she feels safe going home
today. Celeste says that the relationship is like a seesaw, with her and
Perry "swopping" the power with one another. Right now Celeste has
the power because he hurt her. She wonders why she is there at all.
She tells Susi that it will happen again – Perry will hit her and she'll hit
him back. Susi says that Celeste needs to have a plan for when it does
happen again.

Analysis

A domestic violence counsellor tries to get Celeste to see the situation from an objective perspective.

Study questions

1. Is it a general perception that domestic violence doesn't happen in wealthy marriages?
2. Is Celeste in denial about the severity of the situation?

Quotations

"Yes," said Celeste. "It will happen again. He'll hit me. I'll hit him."

Chapter 34

Ed and Madeline are reading in bed when Madeline asks Ed if he has ever been into erotic asphyxiation. He pretends to like it, and to want to try it with Madeline, and she pushes him off. He asks why she is suddenly so interested, and she tells him Jane's story. He is aghast, but then says "silly girls, men like that prey…." Madeline is shocked and accuses him of blaming the victim. She says "what if it was Abigail or Chloe?" They have a huge row, with Madeline insisting that he is being sexist, and she storms out of the room and goes downstairs.

Madeline makes tea and sits on the couch. She realizes her anger isn't so much about the "silly girl" comment, but about Abigail moving out. She also realizes that she does blame Ed for it to a certain extent. It seems that everyone – Ed, Fred and Chloe – have all intruded on her "me and Abigail" thing, and consequently pushed Abigail away.

She goes back to thinking about Saxon Banks and despite her best intentions, she Googles him. She finds who she believes has to be him – a property developer from Melbourne. She looks at the strong-jawed classically handsome man, and hates him on sight for what he did to Jane. What kind of man was this that preyed on innocent young girls? She looked for a resemblance to Ziggy – maybe there was something around the eyes. Then she saw the bio – he has a wife and 3 daughters! Ziggy has 3 half-sisters! She felt a rush of revulsion towards the man.

Suddenly Chloe screams – she's having a nightmare and Madeline rushes off to deal with that.

Analysis
A domestic violence counsellor tries to get Celeste to see the situation from an objective perspective.

Study questions

1. Is it a general perception that domestic violence doesn't happen in wealthy marriages?

2. Is Celeste in denial about the severity of the situation?

Quotations

"Yes," said Celeste. "It will happen again. He'll hit me. I'll hit him."

Chapter 35

Its two weeks before the Trivia Night.

Jane is doing some work on her laptop at Blue Blues and Tom brings her a muffin "on the house". Jane enjoys being at Blue Blues, and Tom is almost starting to feel like a colleague. She's feeling much better in herself too. Was it the book, which awakened sexual desire again? No, she thinks it was telling Madeline the story – it made her realize that her reaction to the words Saxon Banks had said had been too big, or too small. She had become consumed by them. But now it was as if she just wanted to talk about it all the time. She had told Celeste a shortened version during one of their morning walks. The next day Celeste had given her a chain with a lapis stone on it – lapis was meant to heal emotional wounds. Jane thinks that the regular exercise must also be helping – fresh air, exercise and a healing stone.

Jane is "admiring" Tom, and thinking thoughts she hasn't thought in a while, when her mobile rings. It is Mrs. Lipmann, the school principle, asking Jane to go in and see her.

Analysis
Jane is just starting to feel better in herself when the school principal calls to request a meeting with her.

Study questions

What has helped Jane to feel better about herself after such a long time?

Chapter 36

Mrs. Lipmann tells Jane that Renata has complained – Amabella has been a victim of an ongoing spate of bullying. She has various bruises and scrapes, but won't tell anyone who has been hurting her. Mrs. Lipmann says that Miss Barnes has been watching Ziggy, and finds him to be a delightful child. She hasn't seen Ziggy hurting Amabella, but she hasn't seen any other child hurting her either. Mrs. Lipmann tells Jane that the school policy is to help both the bully and the victim, so if they find that it is Ziggy who's been hurting Amabella, he will be helped rather than punished.

She asks Jane if there have ever been any other incidents, at preschool for instance. Jane says there hasn't. Mrs. Lipmann then asks about Ziggy's father and the fact that he is not involved in Ziggy's upbringing. Jane was explaining that Ziggy has many male role models, when Mrs. Lipmann's secretary opens the door. There has been a mix-up and Renata and her husband Geoff are early for their meeting. Renata comes barging in, despite Mrs. Lipmann's and the secretary's protests, and declares that since they are presumably there to discuss the same topic, they might as well do it all together. Renata is yelling at Jane, while Geoff is trying to calm her down and apologize to Jane at the same time. Renata yells: "I want her child to stay the hell away from my daughter."

Analysis
While Mrs. Lipmann is trying to get to the bottom of things, Renata bursts in and yells at Jane.

Study questions

Is Mrs. Lipmann handling things in an acceptable manner?

Chapter 37

Madeline gets home to find Abigail on the couch. She feels out of touch with her, and despairs that she doesn't even know how to be herself around her own daughter. Should she be more like Bonnie? It seems that Abigail prefers Bonnie.

Abigail is busy looking at Amnesty International – she has become very interested in human rights. Bonnie and her mother are members of Amnesty International. Madeline asks Abigail what exactly she is looking at and she replies child marriage and sex slavery. She says the poor girls should be playing with dolls, instead of working in brothels. Madeline feels that Abigail should be playing with dolls or make-up or something instead of worrying about such weighty topics. She felt angry at Nathan and Bonnie, for putting these ideas into her head.

Abigail declares that she is going to do something about the problem. Madeline (with her marketing degree) offers to help her write some letters, but Abigail declares that that would solve nothing – she has an idea.

She gets up to leave – they are going to Bonnie's mother for dinner. Madeline can't resist saying that Abigail hadn't seen *her* mother in weeks.

Analysis
Madeline feels that she is losing Abigail to Bonnie.

Study questions

Is Abigail too young to be worrying about sex slavery and child marriage?

Quotations

"Bye, Mum," said Abigail, and she leaned down to kiss her compassionately on the cheek, as if Madeline were an elderly aunt she'd been visiting and now, phew, it was time to get out of this musty place and go back home.

Chapter 38

Celeste has taken a 6 month lease on a flat in town, and is slowly furnishing it. This is what Susi's plan involves – being ready so that she can take the boys and leave Perry the next time he gets violent.

On a visit to the apartment, she bumps into the woman who lives across the hall, and who has twin daughters.

She gets to thinking about their house, and how it seems to shout "we are wealthy" at anyone who enters. She does not feel comfortable with their money, and their house filled with things that Perry liked. If he didn't like something he would call it cheap and tacky, and she would feel that he was calling *her* cheap and tacky. She had never thought about leaving Perry before – where would she go? But with this apartment she had an escape route. She would get the beds made up for the boys, and stock it with groceries, so it was all ready. But could she really do this to the boys? Take them away from everything they've ever known? She would need to pack a bag and be ready. The next time he hit her, she would leave.

Susi thinks that Perry might try to get custody of the boys, as wealthy fathers often do. His family would get involved. Celeste got to think about the huge extended family Perry had, and how happy he always seemed with them. Sometimes she would watch him interacting with them, and a vision of one of their fights would cross her mind, and she could imagine the disbelief and shame if they were to discover the truth.

She would miss sex with him; sex was never violent even when it followed violence. She would miss living near the beach, and she'd miss his family. Madeline had told her once that when you divorce someone, you divorce their family too. That would be too much to sacrifice, wouldn't it? Celeste was grateful that she could afford to have this place, to have access to money to do this without Perry even realizing. Most women had no back door.

Analysis

Celeste is putting the counsellor's plan into action – an escape route. But would she be able to leave if the time came?

Study questions

1. Should Celeste be setting up the apartment as an escape route, or is that a betrayal of their marriage?
2. Would it be right to take the boys from everything familiar?

Quotations

"It's almost worth it," she'd told Susi. Perhaps it was even fair. A little violence was a bargain price for a life that would otherwise be just too sickeningly, lavishly, moonlit perfect. So then what the hell was she doing here, secretly planning her escape route like a prisoner?

Chapter 39

Ziggy and Jane are on the beach, although it's a miserable cold day. Jane tells him that she saw Mrs. Lipmann and Amabella's mommy the day before. She tells him that someone has been scratching, choking and even biting Amabella. She tells him that Renata thinks it is him. Ziggy just looks off into the distance, saying nothing. "Is it you, Ziggy?" Jane asks. Still he ignores her. She pleads with him, but he just says that he doesn't want to talk about it.

Analysis
Jane tries to find out if Ziggy is the bully.

Chapter 40

Its one week before the Trivia Night.

Madeline is preparing for the book club to arrive. She's not so sure she should have started a book club – was it a reaction to her grief at Abigail moving out? She had chosen a sexy, rollicking book, and the club had somehow gotten the nickname "The Erotic Fiction Club."

Samantha arrives first, and asks Madeline if Jane knows about the petition that is circulating the school – apparently started by Harper and demanding that Ziggy be removed from the school. Madeline is flabbergasted (secretly she wonders if Ziggy did inherit a violent streak from his dad, and if his 3 half-sisters have it too).

Chloe comes in (Ed was meant to be on child duty but has fallen asleep on Chloe's bed). Chloe has overheard the ladies talking about Ziggy and she said Ziggy had been crying that day because Oliver's dad had said that Oliver must stay away from Ziggy because he's a bully. Chloe had punched Oliver over that, which Madeline found hysterical.

Analysis
A petition has been started, urging the school to remove Ziggy for bullying.

Study questions

1. Is it reasonable to kick Ziggy out of school, when it's not known for sure if he is the bully?

Chapter 41

Jane is about to leave for the book club when Miss Barnes calls to tell her about the petition.

Jane has made an appointment with a psychologist for Ziggy. She has asked him over and over if he has been hurting anyone, and he consistently denies it and then says he doesn't want to talk about it.

Miss Barnes is terribly apologetic about the petition, and says that Mrs. Lipmann will be too when she hears about it. Miss Barnes says that she's been watching Ziggy and Amabella like a hawk, even though she has 28 children in the class. She hasn't seen anything happen. Jane is somewhat comforted by the obvious distress in Miss Barnes' voice, but she just doesn't know what to do.

She goes to Ziggy, and finds him crying and asking "is nobody allowed to play with me now?"

Analysis
Things are starting to escalate with the circulation of the petition, even though Ziggy has not been seen hurting Amabella.

Study questions

1. What do you think Miss Barnes and Mrs Lipmann should do about the petition?

Chapter 42

Gwen arrives to babysit the twins while Celeste goes to book club. She has been babysitting since the boys were little. She is quite sarcastic about Perry being away again, then she notices a nasty bruise on Celeste's arm. Celeste tells her that it's a tennis injury – both doubles partners went for the same shot. Gwen is not convinced, and says that it might be time for Celeste to find another tennis partner.

Analysis
The babysitter seems to think that all is not well between Perry and Celeste.

Chapter 43

Ziggy has told Jane that three or four children had told Jane they weren't allowed to play with him. He had wanted to play Star Wars but they had run away from him. He was almost inconsolable, and Jane decides she cannot leave him to go to the book club. She calls Madeline to say that Ziggy is unwell, but she realizes that Jane has found out about the petition. Madeline says how angry she is about it, and ads "Don't worry. We'll fix this."

The babysitter Chelsea arrives, and Jane apologetically pays her anyway even though she is no longer needed. Next thing, Chelsea's mom brings the money back to Jane – they live just downstairs and there's no need to pay Chelsea for not working. She asks if Ziggy's alright, and Jane ends up telling her the story. She can't believe it – she taught children for 24 years and can pick out a bully a mile off. Ziggy's no bully according to her.

Ziggy is still very distressed, so Jane bundles him up and takes him to her parents' house – telling him they'll spend the night and have great fun.

Analysis
Someone else thinks Ziggy is innocent – why is it so hard to prove?

Study questions

1. Do you think little kids have little problems?

Quotations

"I bet it's the parents making the biggest fuss, isn't it?" Irene gave her a shrewd look. "Parents take far too much notice of their children these days. Bring back the good old days of benign indifference, I reckon. If I were you, I'd take all this with a grain of salt. Little kids, little problems. Wait till you've got drugs and sex and social media to worry about."

Chapter 44

Celeste has arrived at book club and is quite disappointed that the book is not being discussed. Everyone is more interested in discussing the petition. They can't believe that Renata would do that when Amabella hasn't actually said outright that it is Ziggy bullying her – Renata is just presuming its Ziggy because of what happened at the orientation day. Can't Renata get a gifted child to say which child is bullying her?

The discussion gets quite heated. Someone suggests that Renata can afford to move Amabella to a private school if she is that concerned. Then all eyes were on Celeste as someone mentioned that Renata and Perry work together. She explained that they were in the same industry, but didn't actually work together. There was also talk about how many of the ladies hadn't yet met Perry as he had been away so much. Celeste said they would all meet him at the trivia night, and she got to thinking how he loved to dress up, and how he had said he would buy her a real pearl necklace in Geneva, for her Breakfast at Tiffany's outfit. She wished he wouldn't – she would rather wear cheap costume jewelry like everyone else would be wearing.

Analysis
The petition threatens to make two camps out of the school parents.

Study questions

1. Would a gifted child be more or less likely to own up to what is happening?
2. Why do you think so?

Chapter 45

Madeline and Celeste are cleaning up after the book club, and chatting about the petition and the fact that nobody who was at the book club would be signing it.

Madeline says that she keeps thinking about Jane and what she went through that night, and now this with Ziggy. Madeline knew that Jane had also told Celeste. Madeline admits that she Googled the man, even though Jane had asked her not to. Celeste said that Jane hadn't mentioned the guy's name to her. When Madeline says "Saxon Banks", Celeste almost chokes on her muffin. She says that Perry has a cousin named Saxon Banks, a property developer with 3 daughters. Celeste is shocked. Madeline calls up his picture on Google, and Celeste agrees that it is Perry's cousin, and she is even more shocked because she *likes* this cousin, finds him very charming. She can't imagine him being unfaithful to his wife, let alone so cruel.

Celeste wonders what she will do if she meets up with him again at a family gathering, and she wonders if she now has a responsibility to say something to Perry. Madeline says that if it was her, she wouldn't be able to keep from telling Ed. Celeste said that she thought it would make Perry angry. "With his bastard cousin? I should think so", says Madeline. No, with her, Celeste counters. Madeline is shocked, but Celeste says that if she tells Perry it would be awkward for him to be around Jane at school functions, and Madeline agrees.

Analysis
Jane's attacker turns out to be Perry's cousin. Celeste has a quandary on her hands.

Study questions

1. Should Celeste tell Perry about Saxon Banks and Jane?
2. Why would it make Perry angry with Celeste?

Quotations

"It might make him angry," said Celeste. She gave Madeline a strangely furtive, almost childish look. "With his bastard cousin? I should think so." "I meant with me." Celeste pulled on the cuff of her shirt.

Chapter 46

As Celeste drives home from book club, she reflects on the last time they had seen Saxon and his wife, Eleni. Perry had been so happy to see Saxon. They were at a family wedding and, having arrived at the reception, Eleni realizes that she has left her phone on the pew in the church. Saxon offers to go back and get it for her, and Perry accompanies him. She can't quite equate the charming, helpful man who would drive back to fetch his wife's phone, with the monster Jane had described. Then she thought about Perry's violent side. Maybe they both had a bad side to them. Genetically speaking they were more than just cousins, as their mothers were identical twins. Had they both inherited something? Or had their mothers somehow "broken" them?

Celeste pondered as to whether she should say something to Eleni. Perry just had a bad temper, but Saxon, it seemed, was pure evil. If he was the one – they weren't 100% sure.

Celeste arrives home to her huge garage, and thinks about the tiny parking space she would have at the apartment if she left Perry. She looks at the bruises on her arm and thinks "Yes, Celeste, stay with a man who does this to you, because of the great *parking*."

Analysis
Celeste ponders Perry's violence and Jane's accusations against Saxon in the light of the fact that their mothers are identical twins.

Study questions

1. Does Celeste have a moral obligation to say anything to Saxon's wife?

Quotations

"She pulled up the sleeve of her shirt and looked at the bruises on her arm. Yes, Celeste, stay with a man who does this to you, because of the great *parking*."

Chapter 47

Jane and Ziggy are at her parents' house. Ziggy is asleep in Jane's old bed, and the adults are discussing the petition, and doing a jigsaw puzzle – a family addiction. Jane was going to give Ziggy the day off school tomorrow.

Jane looks around the kitchen and thinks that perhaps they should leave Pirriwee and go back to her parents. But that makes her think with longing of Blue Blues and Tom, her friendship with Madeline, of her walks with Celeste and going straight from school to the beach with Ziggy in the summer. She realizes how happy they really are. Jane has even picked up 2 new clients.

Jane's father says that they cannot let Renata bully them into leaving the school, especially since it most likely isn't Ziggy doing the bullying. Jane explains that Renata believes it is Ziggy, and that's that.

Jane's mom says that Ziggy is such a sweet child, how could he do such a thing. Jane almost blurts out something about Ziggy possibly inheriting a bad trait from his dad, but saves herself just in time by saying that he was a complete stranger, so one wouldn't know his character. They agree that Ziggy is not and never will be a bully.

Analysis
Jane realizes how happy her and Ziggy are in Pirriwee – how can one woman threaten to ruin everything for them?

Study questions

1. Explain why Jane and Ziggy are so happy in Pirriwee, despite the petition.

Quotations

"And I don't care what sort of personality traits Ziggy's biological father had, I know my grandson, and he is not and never will be a bully."

Chapter 48

Madeline is alone now that Celeste has gone. She doesn't feel like going to bed yet. She feels angry at everyone and everything – Nathan and Bonnie for taking Abigail from her; Renata for the petition and Miss Barnes for letting Amabella be secretly bullied.

She decides to play a game on her iPad to calm herself down. As she often did, she quickly checked on Abigail's Facebook profile. Abigail had changed her profile picture to one of herself in a yoga pose, with one foot on her knee and her hair over one shoulder. One of Abigail's friends had commented on the picture – was it sexy enough for Abigail's' new project, to which Abigail had replied "shhhh – top secret". Madeline typed in – go to bed, it's late, and she has math tutoring in the morning. Abigail replied that Nathan had cancelled the tutor and was going to tutor her himself. In a rage and not caring about the time, Madeline calls Nathan. He asks her if the call couldn't have waited till the morning, as everyone is asleep. Madeline replies that his 14 year old daughter is not asleep, and he should know that. He promises to go check on her and hangs up.

Analysis
Madeline discovers that Abigail is not getting the attention or discipline she needs from Nathan and Bonnie.

Study questions

1. Should a 14 year old girl be allowed to have a Facebook profile?

Chapter 49

Its five days before the Trivia Night.

Jane is walking back from the school library after dropping Ziggy at his classroom. She sees a couple of Blonde Bobs talking about her – one is mimicking her hair pulled back from her face the way Jane wears it, and one was holding a clipboard – clearly the petition. She drops her arm, trying to hide the petition from view. Jane was about to avoid them, when she has a flash back to *the night*, and Saxon Banks' voice in her ear – "never had an original thought in your life, have you?"
She turns back to the women and says that her son has never hurt anyone in his life. One of them tries to interrupt but she repeats herself and walks away.

Jane goes to Miss Barnes' class to do her weekly help with reading. Miss Barnes is pleasantly surprised to see her; she thought that in light of all that was going on, Jane wouldn't have come. Jane jokes with her that she is starting her own petition – for all the children that won't play with Ziggy to be suspended.

Analysis
The two camps of parents are becoming clearly delineated.

Chapter 50

Jane was helping Max with his reading. Parent reading was done out in the playground. He was finished, she complimented him and had some trouble getting him to go back to class, but he eventually obeyed. The next child to come out was Amabella. The first thought that Jane had was about Ziggy and the petition, but then she reminded herself that she had become fond of the quiet, serious little girl, and she vowed that she would not say anything to Amabella about the matter.

Amabella was reading a book about the solar system. As a gifted child, she gave amazingly intuitive answers to Jane's questions – some of which Jane thought she would have to Google to be sure of! Suddenly she found herself talking to the little girl, asking Amabella if she knows that she is Ziggy's mom, and if Ziggy had been hurting her. Amabella starts to cry and mumbles something that sounds like "It wasn't", and Jane says "Is that what you said, it wasn't him?"
Suddenly Harper is standing at the edge of the sandpit, asking Amabella if she is okay, and pointedly ignoring Jane. She continues speaking to Amabella, and calls her out of the sandpit. She accuses Jane of upsetting Amabella. Jane tells her to mind her own business and go gather some more signatures for her little petition. Harper says that she can't leave Jane to keep bullying Amabella, "Like mother, like son!"

Jane kicks at the sand, Harper accuses her of kicking her shin, and a shouting match ensues, which is broken up by one of the fathers who had also been doing parent reading.

Analysis
The bullied child seems to tell Jane that Ziggy is not the bully.

Study questions

1. Should Miss Barnes have sent Amabella out to Jane for reading, given what was going on with the petition?
2. Explain your answer.

Chapter 51

It's the day before the Trivia Night.

It's the Friday assembly at school, and Madeline and Ed are there to watch Fred play his recorder. Ed mentions that the editor of the local paper had emailed him, asking him to do an article on the petition that was going around the school. Ed had been a journalist at the *Australian* but had given it up 3 years ago so that Madeline could go back to work part time, and to help with the children. He was now a reporter on the local paper. Madeline is not happy about him doing the article.

Celeste and Perry arrive – Perry as usual in a handmade Italian suit. Celeste and Madeline hang back, and Madeline asks Celeste if she has told Perry about his cousin. She says no, looking almost frightened. Celeste asks about Jane, but Madeline reminds her that Jane has an appointment with a psychologist for Ziggy, to try and get to the bottom of the bullying.

Perry asks about the petition, and mentions that he "sort of "knows Renata through work. He asks if he should sign the petition if Renata asks him. Celeste says that if he signs the petition, she will leave him. Perry's face hardens, but he makes light of it in front of the others.

Analysis
The petition is working its way into all the families' lives.

Study questions

1. Why would Madeline not want Ed to write the article?
2. Explain why what Celeste says to Perry is careless.

Chapter 52

Madeline and Ed are seated in the school auditorium, with its magnificent ocean view. Bonnie comes in and sits on the aisle seat across from Madeline. Madeline is having a bad PMS Day; Ed puts his hand comfortingly on her knee. It is quite a cool morning, yet Bonnie is wearing a sleeveless vest. Madeline asks her if she is cold, and Bonnie replies that she has just taught a yoga class, so her core body temperature is still high.

Madeline is really unhappy that "this stranger", meaning Bonnie, knows what her daughter had for breakfast while she doesn't know. Bonnie comments on the math tutor saga, and then informs Madeline that Abigail is really developing a social conscience; in fact she no longer wants to be a physiotherapist, she wants to be a social worker. Madeline says that would be a disastrous career for Abigail as she's not tough enough. As the concert begins, Bonnie leans over and whispers to Madeline that they would love to have her and Ed over for Abigail's 15th birthday the following Tues. A guest at her own daughter's birthday party? Wonderful!

Analysis
Bonnie stakes her claim on Abigail.

Study questions

1. Explain how you understand Madeline's reaction to Bonnie's invitation.

Chapter 53

Jane is at the psychologist's with Ziggy. She has assessed Ziggy and is now reporting back to Jane while Ziggy plays in a glass adjoining room. The psychologist says that she doesn't think that Ziggy is a bully, and she doesn't think that he is lying, unless he's the most accomplished liar that she has met. The other option is that he could be a psychopath, which makes Jane almost fall off her chair. But she doesn't think that either. She mentions that Ziggy is obviously suffering from a lot of anxiety and she wouldn't be surprised if he was the one being bullied. She thinks the bullying may be verbal.

The psychologist also mentioned that they had spoken about Ziggy's father, and that he thinks he may be a Storm trooper or Darth Vader – someone dangerous or mysterious. He knows that it upsets Jane to talk about him, and he said that she gets a funny look on her face if he talks about his Dad.

Analysis
A professional announces that Ziggy is not a bully.

Study questions

1. Do you think Ziggy might be getting bullied himself?
2. Why do you think so?

Quotations

"Do I have a funny look on my face?" asked Jane. "A little bit," said the psychologist. She leaned forward and gave Jane a woman-to-woman look of understanding as if they were chatting in a bar. "I take it Ziggy's father was not exactly a good guy?" "Not exactly," said Jane.

Chapter 54

Perry drives Celeste home after the assembly. The boys did very well acting as a croc, and the parents had all enjoyed it. Celeste can see that Perry is pre-occupied and she thinks back to the comment she made about leaving him if he signs the Ziggy petition. She knows he would have been very embarrassed in front of Ed and Madeline. What had come over her? She thinks it must be the apartment, which is now furnished and ready for her and the boys – she had been admiring it yesterday morning, but then last night she had woken with Perry's arm over her and she thought about it all. She had rented and furnished an apartment – what was she thinking?! Perhaps the guilt of it made her say what she did, but then again the thought of anyone signing that petition made her angry – let alone her own husband. He owed a debt to Jane, because of what his cousin had done.

They reach home, and Celeste says she's sorry Perry has to rush off to work, it would have been nice to have some coffee together. He says that actually he needs to get something from the office, so they go inside. As they enter the house, he grabs her hair and twists it painfully, telling her that if she ever embarrasses him like that in front of other people he will kill her. She says that she is sorry, but she obviously didn't say it quite right, because Perry grabs her on each side of her face and smashes the back of her head into the wall. She sinks to the floor, retching. Perry walks off, but returns with some ice wrapped in a tea towel, which he holds to her head. She looks at his pale drawn face as he sobs once, then they rock together in their voluminous entrance hall.

Analysis
Domestic violence is taken to a new level.

Study questions

1. What made Celeste say she would leave Perry if he signed the petition?
2. Describe your feelings as you read about Perry's attack on Celeste.

Quotations

"His features were dragged downward, as though he were being ravaged by some terrible disease. He sobbed once. A grotesque, despairing sound, like an animal caught in a trap. She let herself fall forward against his shoulder, and they rocked together on their glossy black walnut floor beneath their soaring cathedral ceiling."

Chapter 55

Madeline is at work at the Pirriwee Theatre, calling her friend Lorraine to organize advertising in the local paper. Lorraine is the mother of one of Abigail's friends, Petra, and a known gossip. Lorraine asks Madeline if she's heard "the latest", which involves Renata. Madeline thinks she is referring to the petition and launches into a rant, but Lorraine stops her short by saying she's referring to a French matter – the nanny. Madeline says oh yes, apparently the nanny didn't even pick up that the bullying had been going on. Lorraine says forget the petition, she's talking about the nanny and the husband – Geoff. Despite how she feels about Renata, Madeline would not wish this on her. Lorraine says that someone needs to tell Renata before she finds out via the grapevine, but Madeline says she can't be the one to tell her.

Lorraine asks Madeline what the charity thing is that Abigail is doing for Amnesty International. Madeline doesn't know, but Lorraine said that the way Petra was talking about it set off her "mommy alarm" and she thinks Madeline should find out what's going on. Despite knowing Abigail will be in class, Madeline texts her to say "call me as soon as you get this".

Analysis
Something suspicious is going on with Abigail. Madeline needs to find out what.

Quotations

"How sharper than a serpent's tooth it is to have a thankless child, Abigail," she said to the silent phone.

Chapter 56

Celeste is lying in bed, still in shock from Perry's attack. He comes in and offers her more tea, and says that he will work from home for the morning to make sure that she's okay. He has arranged for Madeline to pick the boys up from school, so she must just relax. The ice pack was helping but she was still in a lot of pain. And the shock – it was like he was Dr. Jekyll and Mr. Hyde, but she couldn't remember which of the two was the baddie. He tells her to just call if she needs anything.

Susi had said that the most dangerous time for a battered woman was after she ended the relationship, but could that be true? If he had been just one notch angrier today, he would have smashed her head against the wall again, maybe a bit harder; maybe he would have killed her. If she left him, he would be embarrassed – enough to kill her? It was just so surprising that the man who loved her with all his heart would probably end up killing her.

Analysis
Celeste is in shock, and surprise, that the man who loves her with all his heart will probably end up killing her.

Study questions

1. Is Celeste being overly dramatic thinking that Perry will probably end up killing her?
2. Explain your answer.

Quotations

If she left he would probably kill her. If she stayed, and they remained on this trajectory together, he would probably, eventually, find something to be angry enough about that he would kill her.

Chapter 57

Nathan calls Madeline to tell her that Abigail has set up a website to raise funds for Amnesty International. He sounds very distressed, but Madeline has to yell at him to get him to give her the website address so that she can have a look. Abigail has launched www.buymyvirginitytostopchildmarriageandsexslavery.com." The picture on the front page is the one of Abigail in the yoga pose, which under the name of the website seemed to take on a sleazy character. Madeline berates herself for "raising an idiot". She feels sick. Nathan tells her to look at the comments that have been made – none of them very flattering or charitable. Madeline yells at Nathan that he has to shut the website down – he and Bonnie should have been watching her, so they need to fix this.

Analysis
The truth comes out about what Abigail has been up to while staying with Bonnie and Nathan.

Study questions

1. Should Abigail, at 14, have had the kind of unsupervised internet access that has allowed her to put up the website?
2. Explain your answer.

Quotations

"How the hell did this happen? Why weren't you and Bonnie watching what she was doing? You fix it! Fix it now!"

Chapter 58

After the psychologist's appointment, Jane and Ziggy stop at Blue Blues for coffee. She looks out at the ocean and wonders how their time at Pirriwee could have been so disastrous. The lease on the apartment is up in two weeks' time – perhaps the best thing would be for them to go. She admits to herself that her real reasons for coming here were so messed up, it wasn't a surprise that things hadn't gone well. Her thoughts about Saxon Banks had changed, though – she wasn't quite as obsessed with him and could see him in a clearer light. Perhaps he was the only man who could get past her fertility issues and give her a baby…..

Jane asks Ziggy if he would like to move to a new school, where people will be nicer to him. He says no, he's quite happy – even though some kids aren't allowed to play with him, he has a lot of friends. He starts listing them, and when he gets to Amabella, Jane is shocked. He seems surprised, and explains that Amabella likes Star Wars too, and knows a lot about it, but the teachers won't let her and Ziggy talk anymore. Jane says that's because her parents think its Ziggy that's hurting her, and he says it isn't him. When Jane asks him who it *is*, he shuts down and says he doesn't want to talk about it. Amabella said that if he told anyone, he would be "killed dead". Jane suggests that he writes down the name, because that would not be the same as telling. As she is getting a pen and paper for him, a couple walk into the store.

Harper points Jane out to her husband, Graeme. He comes over and, despite Harper's pleas to leave it, he puts his hands on the table, leans into Jane's face, and threatens to call the police if Jane ever goes near Harper again. Tom comes up with Jane and Ziggy's order, and asks Graeme and Harper to leave the store. They are aghast – they are regular customers – but Tom stands his ground and tells them to leave. Other customers applaud, but Jane is embarrassed that he has lost a customer. Tom comes over to see if Jane is okay. She realizes she loves him – and Madeline and Celeste; that she's made real friends here. But she's made real enemies too, so it would be best to leave.

Tom goes off to see to another customer, and Ziggy tells Jane that he has written down the name of the bully. Jane looks at the pad, where Ziggy has written MaKs. It takes a while for her to register that he means Max. She questions him - Ziggy nodded. "The mean twin."

Analysis
The name of the bully is revealed.

Study questions

1. Should Jane have encouraged Ziggy to write down the name?

Chapter 59

Perry has to leave for work. He has given Celeste a strong painkiller to help her, and she is trying to articulate something. She mentions a time he had spoken of, when he was a little boy and was being bullied, and Saxon had punched the boy's tooth out. She had been thinking of Saxon since the book club night. "Saxon Banks. Perry's hero. Jane's tormentor. Ziggy's father."

She feels that she and Jane had something in common – they had both been hurt by these men. The difference was that Celeste fights back.

She tells Perry that he's not as bad as Saxon – he "wouldn't do that". When Perry asks her what, she can't quite remember, as the pain medication takes over. Perry leaves.

Analysis
In her drugged state, Celeste's mind is trying to make connections.

Quotations

"But you're not as bad as him," she mumbled. Wasn't that the only point? Yes. That was key. That was key to everything. "What?" Perry looked bemused. "You wouldn't do that." "Wouldn't do what?" said Perry.

Chapter 60

Nathan is trying to shut down Abigail's site, but he can't work out her password. Between them he and Madeline try everything they can think of, to no avail. Madeline decides to go and take Abigail out of school and make her shut the site down. She thinks of Abigail, who hasn't even been kissed by a boy, offering up her virginity. She knows Abigail will say "but those girls haven't been kissed by a boy either". Nathan asks Madeline not to yell at Abigail, but she says of course she's going to yell - "She's selling her virginity on the Internet!"

Analysis
Abigail's site needs to be shut down.

Study questions

1. Are Madeline and Nathan over-reacting?
2. Why?

Chapter 61

Jane drives Ziggy back to school. He asks if Jane is going to speak to Max and tell her to stop hurting Amabella. Jane says that probably the teacher would speak to him, and then she gets to thinking how best to handle things. Doesn't she have an obligation to speak to Celeste first and then Mrs. Lipmann or Miss Barnes?

Jane tells Ziggy that he did the right thing by telling her. He's horrified – he never *told* her. She asks him about the orientation day and he explains that Max told Amabella that if she told anyone he had hurt her he would do it again when no one was watching – so she pointed at Ziggy. She had apologized to Ziggy, and he said it was ok. Jane tells him he's a nice boy.

Ziggy seems happy – perhaps a weight off his shoulders? Jane realizes that he hadn't been anxious because he was being bullied – he was anxious because he had been keeping such a big secret. He goes skipping past Mrs. Ponder's house, while Jane is deep in thought as to how Celeste would react when she hears about Max. She's never seen Celeste angry. In fact, she has seemed quite preoccupied lately.

Mrs. Ponder calls out, and starts to chat about the Trivia Night, which Jane had all but forgotten about. Mrs. Ponder said that Jane should have a haircut – a pixie cut. While Jane is thinking about this, Mrs. Ponder notices that Ziggy is scratching his head. She has a look and pronounces that he has nits. Just then Thea walks past, and overhears Mrs. Ponder say that Ziggy is "crawling" with nits.

Analysis
One Ziggy problem seems about to be solved, while another one presents itself.

Study questions

1. What should Jane do with the information about Max?
2. How do you foresee the nits problem playing out?

Quotations

"Nits!" she said with satisfaction in a nice, clear, loud, carrying voice, at the exact moment that Thea came hurrying by, carrying a lunch box. "He's crawling with them."

Chapter 62

Madeline picks Abigail up at school. She's acting like a typical teenager – "whatever" and "I knew it". She doesn't think what she's done with the website is a particularly big deal. Madeline is being very controlled. She tells Abigail that she understands what she is trying to do – a publicity campaign with a 'hook'. Only the hook is a little extreme. Abigail says she is just trying to raise awareness and Madeline says yes, she is raising awareness – about herself. She asks Abigail if she is actually going to go through with it, she's too young to be having sex. Abigail says "so are those little girls".
Madeline tries another tack – they can start an awareness building campaign, make use of Ed's contacts in the journalism world. Abigail declares that she is not giving them the password even if they torture her.

They have arrived at the Pirriwee School pick-up. Madeline is getting heated, yelling at Abigail about having thought it through, has she thought about sleeping with some stranger? She looks over at Abigail and can see that she is trying not to cry. She tells Abigail it will be vile and painful. Abigail yells that it's vile and painful for those little girls. "But I'm not their mother!" shouted Madeline, as she slams straight into the back of Renata's BMW.

Analysis
Madeline has an encounter with Renata.

Study questions

1. Suggest a better campaign for bringing about awareness of child marriage and sex slavery, than what Abigail has done.

Quotations

"And have you thought through what it would be like to have sex with a stranger? To have some horrible man touching you—"

Chapter 63

Following Mrs. Ponder's suggestion, Jane takes Ziggy to Hairway to Heaven, the popular hair salon run by Mrs. Ponder's daughter Lucy. Lucy starts to treat Ziggy, and asks if she should give him a trim while she's busy. Lucy mentions that she should check Jane's hair too, while she's about it, and that her mom wants her to give Jane a pixie cut.

Analysis
Hair salon time.

Chapter 64

Madeline drops the twins off with Celeste, and sees that she looks really ill – could it be a virus or something? She offers to take the boys home with her but Celeste says she'll be alright. Madeline tells Celeste that she ran into Renata's car at school because she was yelling at Abigail, because Abigail is auctioning her virginity on the internet. Celeste is shocked, but Madeline gives her the web address and says she should have a look. Celeste says that at least it's for a good cause. Madeline wonders if the virus is making Celeste delirious. She tells Celeste that she should go lie back down, and when she gets a chance she should check the twins for nits.

Analysis
Celeste is seemingly delirious.

Study questions

1. Does "being for a good cause" make Abigail's website okay?
2. Why?

Chapter 65

Eight hours before the Trivia Night.

Jane is driving back to Pirriwee after dropping Ziggy with her parents, where he'll spend the night while she goes to the Trivia Night. It's raining very heavily. Last week she had told her parents that she wouldn't go, because of all the drama going on, but now that things seemed to be resolving themselves she feels more optimistic. She had told Miss Barnes, who had organized a meeting for first thing Monday morning. She had tried to tell Celeste but she was sick in bed – Jane would need to see her before Monday's meeting. She thought that perhaps some parents would apologize to her. She could stay in Pirriwee and keep working at Tom's.

Jane decided to stop off at Blue Blues before going home. It was raining so hard there was no one else around. She was craving some of Tom's coffee and she wanted Tom to see her new haircut – gay men notice things like that. She reflected on how surprised and pleased her mom had been to see the new do; she realized that she really had neglected her appearance since the night with Saxon Banks. She had no umbrella but decided to make a run for it anyway.

Analysis
Jane feels more optimistic about staying in Pirriwee.

Study questions

1. Describe how you have felt when a seemingly insurmountable problem goes away.

Chapter 66

Celeste woke up to the sound of classical music and the smell of bacon and eggs. Perry must have got up early with the boys to make breakfast – and amends? It was amazing how quickly the forgetting and healing process had begun again. She lay there thinking about the Trivia Night that night. They would dress up as Elvis and Audrey – Perry's costume had come from a very expensive online shop, not the make-do that everyone else would be wearing. They would be the picture perfect couple again.

He was going to Hawaii the next day. This time is was a party, and he had asked her to go with him, but she remembered another such trip where she had embarrassed him and he had hit her. No, she would move herself and the boys to the apartment while he was gone. She would get a family lawyer – there would be a fight, but he wouldn't *kill* her. The boys could still cook breakfast with him when they saw him on weekends.

The boys come running in, announcing that they have made breakfast for her.

Analysis
Celeste makes a tough decision.

Study questions

1. Describe the significance of Perry and Celeste being the picture perfect couple while they have such a destructive marriage.

Quotations

"Yesterday was the last time he would hurt her. It was over."

Chapter 67

Nathan, Madeline and Ed are discussing Abigail's website, which is still very much up. Abigail is on her bed, with head phones on and curled up in a fetal position. Nathan had come around the previous evening and begged and cajoled with Abigail to take the website down. Even when Nathan began to cry with frustration, she was shocked but wouldn't back down. She felt they were making too much of "the sex thing"; she may or may not go through with it but at the moment she was the only voice those little girls had. As if she thought no one else in the world was doing anything.

Ed suggests that they call the Australian office of Amnesty International – surely they wouldn't want to be associated with something like this. Madeline thinks it's a good idea. Just then Chloe and Fred come in shouting at each other. Madeline sorts them out, then sees Abigail leaning against the door. Abigail announces that she has taken down the website. She hands them an email, from Larry Fitzgerald from South Dakota. Larry has seen her website and would like to make a bid, but not for her virginity. If she will close the website down, he will send $100 000 to Amnesty International. Abigail thought that was a large amount of money and that Amnesty could do "something useful" with it. She has taken it down, but will put it straight back up again if he doesn't send her proof of payment.

Abigail goes to the fridge, roots around and finds a Tupperware with spaghetti bolognaise in it. Turns out she's not vegan when she's home with Madeline.

Analysis
Abigail is rescued by a benefactor.

Study questions

1. How do you feel about how easily Abigail gives up the fight?
2. Comment on her being "selectively vegan". What do both these things say about Abigail?

Quotations

"Madeline grinned at Ed and then back at Abigail. You could see the relief coursing through her daughter's young body; her bare feet were doing a little dance as she stood at the refrigerator. Abigail had put herself in a corner, and the wonderful Larry Fitzgerald of South Dakota had given her an out."

Chapter 68

Jane arrives at the door of Blue Blues, sopping wet, to find a closed sign. Tom sees her, however, and invites her in. He had decided to close up and watch TV in his flat as he hadn't had a customer in hours. He takes her through to the flat, and she sees a jigsaw puzzle on the table. He asks where Ziggy is, and she explains that he's with her mom and dad so she can go to the Trivia Night. Tom says that he is also going, he was invited because so many of the school parents are regulars.

She goes into the bathroom and changes out of her wet things and into some sweat pants and a shirt of Tom's. He helps her fold the sleeves up. He remarks on her haircut, and she says that she knew he would notice – gay men always do. He seems a bit surprised, and says he's not gay. She recalls how Madeline had told her about the breakup with his boyfriend, and how devastated he was. Laughing, Tom explains that that was another Tom – a mechanic – but he can understand how she would think he was gay: a barista who cooks and bakes and does jigsaw puzzles. Jane feels really embarrassed. She had practically undressed in front of him, leaving the bathroom door ajar, as though he was a girl. They were both blushing.

Analysis
Jane makes an interesting discovery.

Study questions

1. How would you feel if you had made the same mistake as Jane, regarding Tom?

Quotations

"Their eyes met. His face, so dear and familiar to her now after all these months, felt suddenly strange. He was blushing. They were both blushing. Her stomach dropped as if she were at the top of a roller coaster. Oh, calamity."

Chapter 69

Half an hour before the Trivia Night.

Celeste is getting ready – black dress, hair up, and the pearl necklace Perry had bought her in Switzerland. Josh comes to the door and tells her she looks beautiful. He sits on the bed and asks if he can tell her a secret, because keeping it makes him feel sad. Josh tells her that Max doesn't hurt Amabella anymore, but yesterday he had pushed Skye down the stairs (Skye – Nathan and Bonnie's little waif-like girl). Celeste asks Josh what he means about Max not hurting Amabella anymore, but he is more interested in telling her about Max hurting Skye. In the background, Perry answers Celeste's phone, and Max comes running to tell Celeste he has a wobbly tooth. All Celeste can think of is Susi asking her how Perry's abuse had affected the boys.

Perry comes in, looking so strange in his Elvis wig and suit. Celeste is thinking about what to do – should she call Jane and tell her, or call Miss Barnes………. Perry tells her he has a message for her from Mindy. She doesn't know who Mindy is, so he explains. "Your property manager", he says, adding that they want to put new smoke alarms into the apartment and would Monday morning suit her? Celeste's stomach has plunged.

The doorbell rings.

Analysis
Two interesting discoveries take place. Celeste finds out who the bully is, and Perry finds out what Celeste has been up to.

Study questions

1. Are you surprised that Max is the bully?

2. Why?

Chapter 70

The Trivia Night

Jane arrives at the Trivia Night and is handed a cocktail by a Blonde Bob. She wonders through the crowd of assorted Elvises and Audreys, enjoying the very strong cocktail. All she could think about was "Tom is straight" and "Tom is not gay". She meets Madeline, one of the only women not dressed in black – Madeline is top to toe pink. She has had a couple of the cocktails. She tells Jane that Abigail has shut down the website, asks about the psychologist. Jane can feel the cocktail going to her head, but she tells Madeline that the appointment went well, and that she found out that Ziggy was not the bully. They discuss the nits, which Chloe and Fred have too.

Jane tells Madeline how Graeme had accosted her in Blue Blues, and how Tom had thrown him out. He comes up at that point and Jane throws her arms around him. Madeline berates him for not looking anything like Elvis, but he says he doesn't do costumes. Tom and Jane discuss the cocktails, and Jane realizes that although she had always thought Tom was good looking, she hadn't realized quite *how* good looking. Madeline senses that something has changed.

Ed comes up and puts his arm around her. Look darling, she says *Tom* and *Jane.* Ed is oblivious, but before Madeline can say anymore, Jane says "Look who's here. The king and queen of the prom."

Analysis
While Madeline realizes that something has changed between Jane and Tom, Perry and Celeste arrive at the Trivia Night.

Study questions

1. Why would Jane have described Perry and Celeste as the king and queen of the prom?

Chapter 71

Perry and Celeste are driving to the Trivia Night. She was a bit surprised that they were still going, but then she remembered – they never cancelled. Perry had already posted pictures of them on Facebook. He had turned on the charm when Gwen had arrived to babysit. Celeste watched the windscreen wipers going back and forth, like her mind – Confusion, Clear, Confusion, Clear. She watched Perry's hands on the steering wheel. He was just a man in an Elvis costume driving to a party – wasn't he?

Perry parks the car, and they both sit there, silent. Then Celeste speaks – she says that it is Max that has been bullying Amabella. He asks how she knows and she said that Josh had told her. Perry says he'll speak to the teachers on Monday and Celeste reminds him that he won't be here. He says he'll speak to Max in the morning. She asks what he will say, and Perry says he doesn't know. Then Celeste launches off the precipice and asks Perry if he'll tell Max that's not the way to treat a woman. He starts to shout that the boys have never seen anything, but Celeste says they have – she can recall a couple of times when one of the boys had seen Perry hit her.

Perry asks her about the apartment and when she's planning on leaving. She says next week, while he is away. Perry rests his head on the steering wheel, and his body is convulsing with tears. He looks at her with tears running down his face and says he'll get help – he promises. She tells him he won't, and he admits that he had got a referral from the family doctor to see a psychiatrist, but that he never got around to going. He says he'll get another referral. He just doesn't know what happens to him when he gets angry; he never makes a decision to do something, it just happens. He feels sick about yesterday.

Celeste tells him that they can't bring up the boys like this. She realizes that if Josh hadn't told her tonight about Max being the bully, then she probably still wouldn't have left. But she can't leave the boys with this legacy of violence. She tells Perry that he must know that it's over. He says that he'll do anything, resign, and take some time off, whatever it takes to make it work. Just then a face appears at the window – Renata asking if they need to share their umbrella.

Analysis

Celeste reveals the truth about Max, and what that means for the marriage.

Study questions

1. Is Celeste doing the right thing by leaving Perry, or should she give him the opportunity to get help?
2. Do you believe that Perry will indeed get help? Why?

Quotations

"This is when you should feel fear, she thought. This is not the way Susi said it should be done. Scenarios. Plans. Escape routes. She was not treading carefully, but she'd tried to tread carefully for years and she knew it never made the slightest difference anyway."

Chapter 72

Everybody watched as Perry and Celeste entered the room – like movie stars arriving. Madeline turns and finds Bonnie next to her. Obviously Bonnie doesn't do costumes either. Madeline is trying to be nice, but can feel her PMS wanting to erupt at Bonnie even through the haze of the cocktails. She grabs another two off a passing tray and hands one to Bonnie. A Blonde Bob comes past and announces that the caterer is stuck in traffic because of the rain. And so is the MC, who has all the trivia questions.

Bonnie says that the drinks are going straight to her head. Madeline sees Ed talking to Renata so she tells Bonnie that she needs to rescue her husband from talking to an adulterer, before he gets any ideas. Very bitchy, she then says, speaking of adulterers, where is my ex-husband? Bonnie looks at Madeline with eyes that aren't totally focused and confronts her. She says that Nathan left Madeline 15 years ago and it was time that Madeline forgave him, even though he will never forgive himself. Madeline is quite pleased to be seeing another side of Bonnie. Just then someone behind Bonnie steps back, and Bonnie spills her drink all over Madeline's dress.

Analysis
Madeline can't help being bitchy to Bonnie. Is the spilt drink an accident?

Study questions

1. Do you think Bonnie deliberately spilt the drink on Madeline?
2. Why?

Chapter 73

An hour into the trivia night and there is still no food. The drinks are flowing freely and conversations are starting to get animated. Tom and Jane find themselves smiling at each other frequently, as though they were in their own little world.

Miss Barnes comes tottering up, clearly under the influence of the pink cocktails. She talks to Jane about the "issue" and the Monday morning meeting. She complains that it's not just the petition that is annoying, but how parents keep turning up. Renata has taken a leave of absence from work and keeps appearing at the school to check on things. Jane says it sounds like harassment to her. Miss Barnes continues on about how she has no privacy, and parents feel they can just approach her at any time, no matter where she is or who she's with. She seems quite distressed and goes off to splash her face.

Jane turns to find Tom there, with some Pretzels that someone had found in the kitchen. Jane is feeling so happy, kind of woozy with happiness, and Tom's not gay. Just then Celeste joins them and tells Jane she has to tell her something.

Analysis
The pink drinks continue to loosen tongues.

Study questions

1. Have you ever gone up to a teacher in the shop or somewhere without any thought to her privacy?

Chapter 74

Celeste suggests that she and Jane go out on the balcony to get some air. They walk past Perry chatting to Ed about golf. Celeste can see that he looks fine on the surface, but is drinking more than normal. She knows that by the time they leave for home the repentant man will be gone; she can imagine how his anger is twisting and turning, getting ready to erupt later.

Outside on the balcony it's cool and wet, but Jane thinks it's nice so they decide to stay. Celeste notices how pretty Jane looks with her haircut and her red lipstick. Celeste tells Jane that Josh had told her about Max being the bully. She is so apologetic, but Jane keeps insisting that everything will get sorted out and it wasn't Celeste's fault. Celeste can't help thinking that somehow it might be. Just then Bonnie and Nathan come out onto the balcony. Celeste remembers that Josh had told her that Max had pushed Skye down the stairs. Celeste apologizes to Bonnie but Bonnie says Skye had told her and they had discussed some strategies for if it happened again. Nathan said that they had already emailed Miss Barnes to tell her about it.
Celeste apologizes again, but Nathan says not to worry – they're kids, they have to learn how to share, stand up for yourself, don't hit your friends and all the other things they need to learn to be a grown up.

Analysis
Celeste breaks the truth to Jane, not realizing she already knows.

Study questions

1. Should Celeste feel that she is partly to blame for Max's behaviour?
2. What about Josh, who isn't a bully?

Quotations

"No need to be sorry! Gosh! They're kids!" said Nathan. "They've got to learn all this stuff. Don't hit your friends. Stand up for yourself. How to be a grown-up." "How to be a grown-up," repeated Celeste shakily.

Chapter 75

Madeline manages to extract herself from a boring conversation – she has seen Nathan and Bonnie on the balcony talking to Jane and Celeste, and wants to join them. On her way to the balcony she passes a group of Blonde Bobs, deep in conversation about Renata's nanny and the affair with her husband. Apparently still unaware, Renata has fired the nanny because she missed the bullying. One of the Blondes mentions the petition – it's going to be handed to Mrs. Lipmann on Monday morning. Another comments on Jane's new haircut and how carefree she looks today; if it was her own child that was such a bully, she wouldn't be flaunting herself in public!

As Madeline makes her way onto the balcony, she finds Renata behind her, also wanting to get some air. Renata apologizes for lashing out at Madeline after Madeline ran into her the day before – she tends to lash out when she gets a fright. Madeline jokes with her that she herself has a very placid personality.

Nathan calls out to Madeline that he believes Bonnie spilled her drink all over her; Madeline said lucky it was a pink drink and matched her dress. Nathan goes on to say that he is celebrating the fact that Abigail took the website down – thanks to Mr. Larry Fitzgerald. Celeste makes a remark but Madeline says "you're Larry Fitzgerald, aren't you?" Celeste tries to make out she doesn't know what they are talking about, but Madeline says "you paid $100 000 to Amnesty to make Abigail shut down the website". Nathan is shocked and asks how they could ever repay her; she replies that she doesn't know what they are talking about, but anyway Madeline saved Max's life, which is a debt that can't be repaid.

They hear shouting coming from inside the hall. Renata says she may have started some little fires – apparently her husband wasn't the only one who thought he was in love with Juliette, the French nanny. Celeste tells Renata that she found out that it was Max bullying Amabella, not Ziggy. Renata asks if she's sure, as Amabella picked Ziggy out on orientation day. Celeste says she is quite sure. Renata claps her hand to her mouth, turns to Jane and says she owes her a huge apology. And Ziggy. She doesn't know what she can do to apologize enough. Jane says apology accepted.

Ed and Perry appear outside. Ed says that things are getting a bit heated in there. He and Perry bring some bar stools over. Renata greets Perry; Celeste notices she is not so kindly towards him now that she knows it's his son that has been bullying her daughter. Nathan introduces himself to Perry – they hadn't met yet. Celeste introduces Bonnie, and Jane – Ziggy's mother. Celeste and Madeline's eyes meet and they both know they are thinking the same thing – Perry's cousin is Ziggy's dad.

Nathan starts to go on about Celeste paying $100 000 to Amnesty to make Abigail close down her site. Perry asks if this is another of his wife's secrets – she seems to have a few of those lately. Celeste sat on her barstool with her hands in her lap, hardly moving. Her face was turned slightly away from Perry, and suddenly Madeline had a realization – this wasn't the perfect marriage or the perfect life – pieces of a puzzle kept coming together.

Perry removes his wig, and starts going on about how Celeste doesn't earn a cent, but knows how to spend it. Renata tries to remonstrate. Only Madeline hears Jane say to Perry "I think we've already met." She tips her head back and repeats herself. Perry says really, are you sure? "I'm sure," said Jane. "Except you said your name was Saxon Banks."

Analysis
Truths keep spilling out. The evening is about to get interesting.

Study questions

1. Is Celeste acting recklessly, giving away so much of Perry's money, and letting Nathan go on about it?

Quotations

"Madeline felt her heart speed up. Something was falling into place. Pieces of a puzzle forming a picture. Answers to questions she didn't know she had. The perfect marriage. The perfect life. Except Celeste was always so flustered. A little fidgety. A little edgy."

Chapter 76

At first Perry appears neutral, like this has nothing to do with him. He doesn't recognize her, but Jane can see that he recognizes what she represents – she was one of many. She never thought to think that he had given a false name.

Celeste turns to Perry. A flicker of a memory that had been playing at the edges of her mind, suddenly came into focus. She recalled the wedding, when Saxon and Perry had driven back to the church to fetch Eleni's phone. When they got back, they were all sitting around sharing stories of Saxon and Perry's shared childhood. One story involved Perry stealing an ice-cream from a store, and when the owner caught him he said his name was Saxon Banks. The store owner called Saxon's mom, and she confirmed that her son was right there. So funny. "It didn't mean anything," said Perry to Celeste.

Jane felt Perry dismiss her as he turned away to face Celeste. She didn't mean anything to him, a distraction, and a fetish. She tells Perry that she moved to Pirriwee because she thought he might be here – she had seen a brochure for the house they now owned, and had asked him if he was buying it. Ever since that night, she had reacted emotionally when she heard the words Pirriwee Peninsular, until one day she had brought Ziggy here. Why had she come? Did she want to see him again? No – she wanted him to see Ziggy, to marvel at his beautiful son. She told herself that she had come here on a whim, not to see Saxon, and it had become true. She hadn't even mentioned to Madeline when she told her the story; she'd forgotten about the brochure, she had come on a whim. And Saxon wasn't even around. Except that now he was – Celeste's husband Perry. He must have been married to Celeste at the time. She felt herself flush with humiliation.

Perry tells Celeste it meant nothing. She says that it meant something to Jane. She was furious – she had thought he was a nice man with a bad temper, but he wasn't. She starts shouting at him, and he says they should discuss it at home and not make a spectacle of themselves. She shouts at him that he's not even looking at Jane, and throws her half full glass of champagne in his face. His hand comes up in a sweeping arc and hits Celeste across the face, causing her head to fling back, and her body to land in a heap on the balcony.

Madeline rushes to Celeste. Celeste sits up and says she's fine, although she's rubbing her face. Madeline looks at the scene. Ed is standing in front of Perry with his hand up, saying Whoa, Whoa. Jane has dropped her glass. Renata is saying she is going to call the police. Bonnie shakes free from Nathan and approaches Perry. "You've done that before", she says to him. Perry is most worried about Renata, who is now on the phone. Bonnie's voice is rough, like a smoker's voice, a fighter's voice. She carries on shouting at Perry – saying that's why his little boy has started hurting girls, because he's seen his daddy hurting his mom. Perry says that his children haven't seen anything. Bonnie rages on, that they've seen, that we all see, and she shoves Perry's chest with both hands. He falls over the balcony.

Analysis
Perry is revealed as Saxon Banks – did Jane come to Pirriwee hoping to find him?

Study questions

1. At what point do you think Celeste realises what Perry did to Jane?
2. Why is Perry most worried about Renata?

Quotations

"Because he's seen what you do. Your little boy has seen you do that, hasn't he?" Perry exhaled. "Look, I don't know what you're implying. My children haven't 'seen' anything." "Your children see!" screamed Bonnie. Her face was ugly with rage. "We see! We fucking see!" She shoved him, both her small hands flat on his chest. He fell.

Chapter 77

Madeline couldn't stop thinking "what if" – if the stool had been shorter or the balcony higher, if he hadn't been drinking……….

Celeste had seen the expression on Perry's face when Bonnie shouted at him – the same cocky expression he wore when he started to get angry with her. She saw him flip over the balcony, then he was gone.

Bonnie had dropped down and curled herself into a ball. Nathan was saying no, no, no.

Jane is in shock – it all happened so fast. She realizes that the shouting from inside the hall is getting louder.

Celeste is staring at the space where Perry had been sitting.

Ed is leaning over the balcony. He yells at Renata to call an ambulance. She says yes, but then she says "I didn't see anything, I didn't see what happened".

Madeline was looking at Nathan. He looked totally distraught. She said that she also hadn't seen what happened – she had been looking inside. Ed can't believe this! But Madeline reiterates that she didn't see anything.

Jane feels the anger like molten gold. She turns to Ed and says that she was also looking inside – she didn't see anything.

Celeste stands up. "I didn't see a thing," she said, and her voice sounded almost conversational.

Ed shouts at everyone to stop it, and he looks terrified.

Celeste walks to the edge of the balcony. She tells Renata that she can call the ambulance now, and then she starts to scream.

Renata is talking into the phone, saying there has been an accident, a man has fallen over a balcony.

Madleline goes to Jane and asks her if it was Perry who...... Before Jane can answer, two fighting Elvises slam into Jane and Madeline, sending them flying in opposite directions. Jane falls awkwardly and feels a sharp pain in her shoulder. As she lies there she can feel the cold wet balcony on her cheek, and hear Celeste's screams and the soft sound of Bonnie crying.

Analysis
Everyone seems to have "not seen" what happened to Perry.

Study questions

1. Why does everyone decide to say they didn't see what happened?
2. What implications could this have for them?

Quotations

Celeste walked to the edge of the balcony and put her hands on the railing. She looked back at Renata and said, "Call the ambulance now." Then she began to scream. It was easy after all those years of pretending. Celeste was a fine actress. But then she thought of her children and she didn't need to pretend anymore.

Chapter 78

The morning after the Trivia Night.

Ed is sitting at Madeline's hospital bed. Her ankle is broken after the two dads collided into her and Jane – she will be having surgery that afternoon.

Madeline is silently berating herself for missing out on what had been going on with Celeste – had Celeste ever tried to tell her something and she'd interrupted?

Ed mentioned that Bonnie had brought round a vegetarian lasagna, and Madeline remembers – Bonnie – the woman everyone is supposedly protecting. Madeline says it was an accident, Ed says, yes so why don't we all just tell the truth. Renata had started the whole thing of pretending she hadn't seen anything. She had probably felt like pushing Perry over the edge herself; Bonnie just got there first. Madeline wondered what would have happened if Renata hadn't said "I didn't see him fall". Would she, herself, have thought of the consequences for Bonnie? Was it an unspoken agreement between the six women on the balcony? Was it justice for every rape, every act of adultery?

Ed says he couldn't live with lying to the police, and Madeline asks if he hadn't already done that last night. He says he was drunk, and anyway the police are going to re-interview everyone involved.

Nathan arrives. He mentions that Abigail has decided to move back home to help Madeline after her op. He says she was just looking for an excuse to move back – the novelty had worn off. Ed wants to leave but Nathan asks him to stay. He starts to explain that Bonnie had a very violent childhood and witnessed her dad doing awful things to her mom. He died of a heart attack before Nathan met her, and Bonnie is still suffering from PTSD.

Madeline says he doesn't have to tell them any of this, but he insists. He goes on to say that Bonnie is a good person. Madeline realizes that he is calling back to the past, to ask the old Madeline for a favor. She thinks of how, regardless of what he did to her, he is still family, still Abigail's father.

Madeline says that they aren't going to say anything to the police that they didn't see what happened. Ed gets up and leaves without a word.

Analysis
The collusion continues. Did Bonnie intend to kill Perry?

Study questions

1. In what way could the collusion be justice for every rape, every act of adultery?
2. Why is Ed so upset that he leaves?

Quotations

"We're not going to say anything to the police," said Madeline. "We didn't see what happened. We didn't see a thing."

Chapter 79

The policeman is questioning Jane in her hospital room. She says that she wasn't sure what happened, it was so noisy, and the champagne cocktails had made everyone drunk. The policeman asks her where she was standing in relation to Perry, and she says she was off to one side.

She thinks back to when she saw Perry take his wig off and become Saxon Banks. She hadn't had a chance to tell him that he was Ziggy's dad, or to hear his apology. Gosh, did she actually think he would apologize? Had that been the reason she had come to Pirriwee? To hear him apologize?

The policeman asks her how well she knew Perry. She says that they had just been introduced. The policeman asks her if she is lying.

Analysis
Jane confronts her reasons for moving to Pirriwee.

Study questions

1. What may have happened if Perry hadn't removed his wig?

Chapter 80

Celeste's mom is with her and the boys, who had cried when she told them about her dad.
Her mom says there is someone called Bonnie at the door. She has brought a vegetarian lasagna and would like to speak to Celeste.

Celeste finds her waiting in the living room. She can't imagine this gentle, caring person lashing out like she did last night. Bonnie says that she can't begin to know what to say – sorry will never be adequate. Celeste says it was an accident. Bonnie asks after the boys and agrees that they wouldn't fully understand yet what is happening.

Bonnie takes a deep breath and tells Celeste that she is going to the police to tell them exactly what happened. Celeste says she doesn't need to, that no one is going to say anything, they'll all say they didn't see what happened. Bonnie explains that she was going to lie to the police – she's had a lot of practice lying to the police, social workers – anyone she had to. She had picked up Skye from her mom's house that morning and remembered the last time she had seen her father hit her mother. She was twenty years old and had run and hid under the bed, which was what her and her sister had always done. Suddenly she realized that she was a grown woman, and didn't need to hide anymore, so she got out and called the police.

Bonnie says "I don't hide under the bed anymore. I don't keep secrets, and I don't want people to keep secrets for me." She reckons that she could lie to the police, so could Madeline and Renata, but Jane wouldn't be able to and neither would Ed. And poor Nathan would be the worst of all. Celeste says she would have lied for her – she can lie. Bonnie says she believes that, but Celeste can stop lying now.

Analysis
Bonnie decides to tell the truth about what happened.

Study questions

1. Do you think Bonnie was brave to decide to tell the police the truth?

Quotations

"I don't hide under the bed anymore. I don't keep secrets, and I don't want people to keep secrets for me."

Chapter 81

Madeline gets a text message from Celeste to say that Bonnie is going to tell the truth – no one needs to lie for her. She quickly calls Ed and catches him just as he is going into the police station. She tells him that Bonnie is going to tell the truth, and he doesn't need to lie. Ed sounds like he is crying. He said that she had asked a very hard thing of him – to lie to the police as a favor to her ex-husband. She says she is so sorry. Ed says he was going to do it, for her.

Ziggy gets a letter from Renata to say that Amabella is having a special party to say goodbye to everyone before they leave to live in London. She would like Ziggy to be the special guest. The theme is Star Wars.

Analysis
Ed is saved from telling the police a lie. Ziggy gets his reward.

Study questions

1. Do you think Ed would have lied to the police for Madeline?

Quotations

"No, you weren't, my darling, she thought as she brushed away her tears with the back of her hand. No, you weren't."

Chapter 82

Four weeks after the Trivia Night.

Tom and Jane are taking a picnic around the headland. There is a journalist sitting in Blues, trying to interview everyone who was involved on the Trivia Night. Tom thinks she is trying to get a book deal together. He says he tells her he's got nothing to say.

Jane thinks back to how her walks with Celeste had begun at the steps to the headland. She's hardly seen Celeste since the funeral. The school had tried to advise parents as to whether to let their children attend the funeral. Jane had let Ziggy go. She didn't know if she would ever tell him that the first funeral he had been too had been his dad's, but at least she had left the option open. Perry's family had been grief-stricken. They had shown a movie of the Perry everyone thought they knew – the good dad, the dashing, charming husband. Jane tried to reconcile that man with the monster in the hotel room, but eventually decided to rather remember the movie – it as better manners. Jane hadn't seen Celeste since the funeral. She hadn't seen Celeste cry at the funeral, although her eyes were puffy and bloodshot.

Jane and Tom keep walking. This is her first bit of exercise since she'd broken her collarbone that night. She wonders about her and Tom. They had seen quite a bit of each other, and had been on a dinner & movie date the week before, but nothing had *happened*. Were they destined to just be friends? They're sitting on the bench and Tom pretends to get a message from Victor Berg, the guy the bench had been dedicated to. "Vic says if I don't hurry up and kiss this girl, I'm a bloody fool." Before Jane can say a word, Tom is kissing her breathless. When she comes up for air, she tells him she was worried they were destined to just be friends, and he says "Are you kidding? Besides, I've got enough friends."

Analysis

As everyone starts to move on with their lives, Tom and Jane start a new life together.

Study questions

1. How do you feel about Ziggy going to Perry's funeral?

Chapter 83

Some of the parents, including some Blonde Bobs, have been talking to the journalist. They remark how all the parents are being incredibly nice to one another now. The school has cancelled the spring ball and will be sticking to cake sales from now on. Harper is giving Graeme another chance, after he also slept with the French nanny.

The detective is pondering over how all his instincts had been telling him it was the wife.......

Analysis
The parents seem to have joined forces again, but there won't be any more alcohol-fuelled fund raising events.

Chapter 84

A year after the Trivia Night.

Celeste is waiting to speak to an audience. She had spoken in court a few times, but this was different. Susi said it would be good for her to speak about her experiences, and it would help other victims.

Celeste had spent a year fighting conflicting emotions. Every time she cried over Perry's death she felt it was a betrayal of Jane. She felt wrong feeling sad for the twins having lost their dad when there was another little boy who didn't even know he was Perry's son. She had dreams in which she hit Perry again and again, yelling "how could you!" She had spent a lot of time with Susi, working through how she could still love Perry, how maybe it was all her fault.

There was a man sitting waiting for his turn to talk. He seemed like a nice gentle man, and he was obviously very nervous.

She thought about Madeline and how much she had done for her over the past year. Madeline still berated herself, saying she should have *known* what was going on.

She thought about the boys – she had a weekly meeting with their teacher to help them all work through the behavioral problems they were having. They had not coped well with their father's death.

Bonnie didn't have to go to jail. The judge took into account that she was not a violent person and never had a criminal record; he took into account the height of the railing (apparently below standard), the unsuitability of the bar stool for that use, and the intoxication of both parties. Bonnie was sentenced to 200 hours of community service, which she served with grace.

Celeste had sold the house and moved into the apartment with the boys. They boys had generous trust funds, but she was determined they were going to learn to earn their own money. She had set up an identical trust fund for Ziggy. Jane had said that wasn't necessary, but Celeste had said that if Perry had known about Ziggy he would have wanted him to have it. There was a moment when Celeste started to say "Perry was....." but couldn't continue, and Jane said "I know he was.....", as if she did know the various sides that had made up Perry.

Susi calls Celeste to the lectern and she realizes that the nice gentle man was also a victim, like her. She searches for a friendly face in the audience, whom she can concentrate on. "This can happen to anyone." she says.

Analysis
Celeste is learning to live life without Perry.

Study questions

1. Do you think Perry would have wanted Ziggy to have the same as the twins, if he had known about him?
2. Do you think Bonnie's sentence was fair?

Quotations

"This can happen to anyone."

Critical reviews

Reviewers have heaped praise on "Big Little Lies" and its author Liane Moriarty. Primarily the praise centers around an intriguing story line, expertly handled by Moriarty in a chatty style that introduces many central characters and keeps the reader interested by bouncing back and forth in the various characters' lives.

The New York Times said:

Ms. Moriarty's long-parched fans have something new to dig into. And her publisher would like to indicate, as clearly as possible, that "Big Little Lies" is more of the same."

The Washington Post's reviewer said:

The cover art for Liane Moriarty's "Big Little Lies" flaunts an oversize, multicolour lollipop shattering into a thousand pieces. It's a perfect metaphor for the seemingly sweet lives of the novel's characters and how the sugar-coated lies they hide behind are smashed to bits.

Entertainment Weekly:

Praise for Moriarty seems to come with a faintly condescending asterisk, probably because her books do, in the broadest sense, fit the label "chick lit." But more than anything she feels like a humanist: a writer whose insights aren't any less wise or funny or true just because she sometimes likes a champagne metaphor or hangs her story on a shoe.

This reviewer's perspective

Big Little Lies is a work of art. Reading it was almost like watching a tapestry come to life as each different colour is added. Liane Moriarty weaves a complex tale, zooming in and out of the central characters' lives, and keeping the reader engaged throughout.

Moriarty's treatment of a social scourge – domestic violence and bullying at schools – is humorously handled. Madeline is such a larger-than-life character, who Moriarty seems to use as a backdrop for the "lesser" characters to shine against.

There is a twist in the tail, which keeps the reader hanging on to the very end. A thoroughly readable book, that entertains as it causes one to consider the social evils that are often hidden behind the most unlikely of places.

Glossary

Bonnie – an interesting character. Bonnie is a vegan yoga instructor, married to Nathan (Madeline's ex-husband). Together they have Skye, a very shy waif-like five year old. Bonnie seems very sweet and gentle on the surface, but when past hurts are recalled, she turns out to have a dark and violent side to her.

Celeste – a very beautiful woman (so beautiful she can get away with wearing no makeup), Celeste harbours a dark secret in the form of her husband's violence. She seems constantly flustered, and no one can imagine why she should be, as she has such a seemingly perfect marriage to a handsome wealthy man. She turns out to be a strong person, who copes well with all that life throws at her.

Ed – a humorous, sweet man. Married to Madeline, he has given up a high-powered job as a journalist to assist Madeline in raising their children. He keeps volatile Madeline on a (mostly) even keel, and is often the voice of reason in a group.

Jane – single mother of Ziggy, who was conceived during a violent and devastating one night stand, which has left Jane haunted by the memories. She is doing a good job of bringing up her little boy, and shows remarkable maturity in dealing with the older mothers, some of whom treat her very badly. Every reader will be happy when Jane finds love with Tom at the end of the book.

Madeline – the central character; friends with Celeste and Jane. Madeline loves conflict, and can be very outspoken. She adds humour and an element of surprise to many scenes. It is Madeline about whom one thinks "she didn't just say that, did she?" Madeline is married to sweet Ed; she was previously married to Nathan, who left her when their daughter Abigail was only 3 weeks old. She has never quite forgiven Nathan, and now has to deal with him and his new wife Bonnie as they have moved into the area and will be sending their five year old daughter to the same school as Madeline and Ed's five year old daughter.

Nathan – Madeline's ex-husband. He is now married to Bonnie, with whom he has a five year old daughter, Skye. Nathan and Madeline's fourteen year old daughter Abigail elects to move in with him and Bonnie, which angers her mother and opens the door for Abigail to perform a rather outrageous teenage stunt.

Renata – a businesswoman and mother. Renata has employed a French nanny to look after her children while she is at work. A self-assured, outspoken person, Renata starts a petition to have Ziggy removed from the school as she believes he is bullying her daughter. She makes a few enemies along the way, but turns out to be not such a bad sort in the end.

Ziggy – five year old son of Jane. He turns out to be a very sweet, well-adjusted little boy who handles being branded a bully, along with the burden of the secret of who the real bully is, very admirably.

Recommended reading

Accidents of Marriage by Randy Susan Meyers

Published September 2nd 2014 by Atria Books

ISBN 1451673043 (ISBN13: 9781451673043)

The Secret Life of Violet Grant by Beatriz Williams

Published May 27th 2014 by Putnam Adult

ISBN 0399162178 (ISBN13: 9780399162176)

One Plus One by Jojo Moyes

Published July 1st 2014 by Pamela Dorman Books (first published January 1st 2014)

ISBN 0525426582 (ISBN13: 9780525426585)